HALF MOON
RANCH

GUNSMOKE

JENNY OLDFIELD

Illustrated by
Paul Hunt

Hodder
Children's
Books

a division of Hodder Headline

**With thanks to Bob, Karen and Katie Foster, and to the staff and
guests at Lost Valley Ranch, Deckers, Colorado**

Copyright © 2000 Jenny Oldfield
Illustrations copyright © 2000 Paul Hunt

First published in Great Britain in 2000
by Hodder Children's Books

A Catalogue record for this book is available from the British Library

ISBN 0 340 75731 0

Typeset by Avon Dataset Ltd, Bidford-on-Avon, Warks

Printed and bound in Great Britain by
The Guernsey Press Co. Ltd, Channel Isles

Hodder Children's Books
a division of Hodder Headline
338 Euston Road
London NW1 3BH

1

'Kids!' Matt Scott grumbled. 'The whole ranch is overrun with them.'

'Maybe that's because it's Kids' Week!' Kirstie fired back. She'd led a couple of horses into the corral and tethered them ready for saddling. 'Y'know – kids sign up and come along to Kids' Week. It kinda figures!'

'Yeah!' Matt smoothed out a striped saddle pad then slung the saddle over Cadillac's broad back. 'But do they have to fool around? Why can't they walk and talk nice and slow, instead of running and yelling all the time? They're spooking the horses out in Red Fox Meadow and really bugging me!'

'Woo-oooh!' Kirstie teased. She too was busy buckling cinches and checking stirrups. Her brother was twenty years old, going on fifty. 'What's eating you? You sound like Hadley!'

'No way!' Matt denied the similarity between himself and the sometimes sour-faced old wrangler who lived with them at Half-Moon Ranch.

'Yeah, you do. And y'know, Hadley can't crack a smile or pay a compliment to save his life!'

Matt peered at her over the curved leather horn of his horse's saddle. 'Are you saying I'm no fun?'

'Not like Brad, you're not.' Kirstie enjoyed the sudden, sullen scowl on Matt's face. Man, was he easy to wind up! 'Brad's always kidding along. You can fool around with Brad. Like, for instance, Jimmy and Taryn and a couple of the others threw him fully-clothed into the hot-tub after they all got back from the trail-ride yesterday.'

'Yesterday was five degrees below zero. We had two inches of snow,' Matt reminded her.

'Exactly. That's why the kids thought Brad needed a dip in the hot-tub! Anyways, this isn't about the weather. It's the fact that you don't like

Brad either.' She ticked a list off on her fingers: 'You don't like kids. You don't like Mom's boyfriend . . .'

'Cut it out, Kirstie!' Matt turned his back on her to concentrate on sliding Cadillac's bridle over the horse's long, aristocratic nose.

'Yeah, cut it out, Kirstie!' Sandy Scott added, coming up unexpectedly behind them. She stood hands on hips, her slim figure well wrapped up in a red fleece jacket which set off her long, fair hair. 'Who said anything about Brad and me being an item?'

'Oops!' Kirstie grimaced. 'Me and my big mouth!'

'You and your wild imagination!' her mom corrected, raising an eyebrow at Matt. 'Brad's here to train our young dude visitors in horseback riding; period!'

'Yeah, yeah!' Brad Martin was Colorado's reining expert, a runner-up with his beautiful black-and-white paint horse in this season's national competition. He was also tall, dark and handsome. And Kirstie knew that he and Sandy definitely had a thing going.

She didn't mind, but Matt did. He tried not to, for Sandy's sake, but a shadow came over his expression every time he set eyes on the champion's flashily dressed, high-booted cowboy figure. Kirstie supposed it must be a mother–son thing.

'Look, can we change the subject?' Matt insisted. He'd saddled up his thoroughbred mount and was ready for action. 'Which group am I leading today?'

'You and Brad can take Intermediates and Advanced both together on the same ride.' Sandy ignored Matt's frown. Instead, she cast an eye over the bunch of noisy kids playing basketball on a roughly marked out area beyond the barn. There was plenty of hollering to be given the ball, then a wild cheer every time it dropped through the basket.

'That leaves me with Beginners,' Ben Marsh, the head wrangler, commented as he passed by leading Navaho Joe. 'Can I take Kirstie along? I reckon I'll need the help.'

'Sure.' Sandy agreed that it would be a good idea. 'The weather's fine, so you can take them along Coyote Trail as far as Whiskey Rock. If you get any stragglers, Kirstie can turn them around and bring them back early.'

'It may be fine now, but there's a storm brewin''

up later.' Hadley walked by on the far side of the fence, his old legs bowed from years in the saddle. He wore his battered white stetson pulled well down over his eyes and didn't alter his loping stride to deliver the bad news.

'Gee, thanks, Hadley!' Kirstie breathed.

'Tell the kids to pack their slickers. If it rains, they just have to cowboy up!' her mom insisted. Seeing Brad come out of the barn with Little Vixen, she waved brightly and went to talk with him.

Meanwhile, out of the corner of her eye, Kirstie saw Hadley walk across the yard to greet Chuck Perry, the farrier who had just screeched to a halt in his dirty white pick-up van. Chuck was a reckless driver, but a mean shoer of horses at forty dollars a time.

Checking the board outside the tack-room she noted that four horses were due to be cold-shoed, including her own palomino horse, Lucky, and a new arrival to the ranch; a pretty blue roan called Gunsmoke.

Normally Kirstie would enjoy watching the small, strong-armed guy with the black moustache at work. Chuck would swivel the peak of his baseball cap round to the back of his head, tie on his leather apron, then slide out his heavy toolbox from the Ford. He'd carefully set up his anvil, his hoof-stand, hammers and nails. Then it would be time for Kirstie to lead a horse into a stall and for Chuck to prise off the worn-out shoes.

But today, because of Ben's large and unruly group of Beginner riders, she would have to leave the assistant farrier's job to Hadley. And she would be riding Jitterbug while Lucky got himself a new set of shoes.

'Advanced and Intermediate riders, all mount up!' Brad was calling to the basketball players. 'Today we climb to 12,000 feet and circum-navigate Eagle's Peak. Any involuntary dismount incurs an automatic penalty!'

'What's the penalty, Brad?' Cory Shaw called as she vaulted the corral fence and headed for her horse, Rodeo Rocky. Cory had been riding horses back home in Texas since she was a little kid of four. A small blonde girl of thirteen with a face full of freckles from a summer in the sun, she had a way with Rocky that Ben and Brad had been able to spot the second she climbed into the saddle.

'Involuntary dismount leads to involuntary hot-tub when we get back to the ranch!' the trainer joked. 'Then involuntary absence from supper, followed by involuntary early bedtime!'

'You can't do that!'

'Our folks paid good money for us to come here this fall!'

'We're not babies!' came the raucous protests.

'Tough!' Brad sat astride Little Vixen, who pranced and strutted her stuff in front of the gathering crowd. She shimmied and danced sideways on a tight rein, picking up her feet and swishing her long, silky tail.

Cocking his hat forward, Brad handled the lively horse with ease. He wore a bright blue shirt underneath a heavy, black hide jacket. His silver spurs glinted on his black-and-red, Cuban-heeled boots.

Matt sat silently beside him on Cadillac, a dour figure in faded denims and dusty brown boots.

'Enjoy!' Sandy waved ironically at her son, then went inside to catch up on paperwork.

As the better riders slowly filed out from the corral, up the dirt track towards Hummingbird Rock, Kirstie turned to help Ben with the Beginners.

They were a motley group of mostly city

kids who had never seen an American quarter-horse in their lives before. However, arriving two days earlier on the Saturday, they'd mostly come across with the tough, no-horse-can-scare-me act.

But show them a deep leather saddle and a chunky wooden stirrup, then you got a different story. Their legs had turned to jello; their whole bodies had started to shake.

'Remember, a horse is twelve hundred pounds of muscle with a brain the size of a can of corn!' Ben had issued the wrangler's favourite warning. 'These animals are strong, OK? They can buck you off any time they want.

'Only, here at Half-Moon Ranch, we train 'em to be nice and gentle. Silver Flash, Johnny Mohawk, Yukon, Snowflake – they're all kid-broke. So long as you follow the rules, I reckon you'll all come out of this week without breaking too many bones!'

Then, on the same day, he'd divided the visitors into groups and assigned them a suitable horse. Beginners on steady rides like Yukon, more experienced riders on the horses with an independent streak, like Navaho Joe and Hollywood Princess. And by today, Monday, everyone had got over their jitters and settled into the saddle.

'OK, Jimmy, you and Crazy Horse lead off up by the cabins, along the forest trail!' Ben called.

He and Kirstie were still checking cinches in the corral as a gum-chewing, mouthy boy from Missouri tried to kick his laid-back mount straight into a trot.

Crazy Horse hunkered down and refused to move, so Kirstie jumped into the saddle and went to help out. She and Jitterbug passed a bunch of horses milling about purposelessly by the exit to the corral, including a nice little black-and-white paint called Taco, ridden by a pretty girl called Taryn. Taryn was also asking none too politely for her horse to trot on.

'No need to pull her mouth around like that.' Kirstie pointed out that Taryn was giving the horse mixed signals. 'Too much contact on the reins makes her pull back, while kicking the heck out of her says "go ahead". Now she don't know what you want her to do.'

'Huh. Stupid horse.' The girl muttered her reply loud enough for everyone to hear.

Ignoring her, Kirstie pushed past and went to show Crazy Horse the way. She noticed a kid called Lacey move her horse, Squeaky, out of the way and give her a shy smile as she passed. Kirstie grinned back.

'Hey, Jimmy,' she said quietly but firmly. 'There ain't no way you're gonna get Crazy Horse to trot up by the cabins. He's smart, see? He knows a bunch of horses trotting up that dirt track only raises the dust. And dust gets inside cabins, then there's a whole lot more cleaning to be done!'

'Huh!' Jimmy's reply echoed Taryn's. He sulked as Jitterbug took over and he and Crazy Horse had to fall into line behind. If they thought he was gonna stay there, they'd another think coming!

'No overtaking at a competitive gait!' Ben yelled out to Jimmy for what must have been the fifth time.

The boy from Missouri was pushing Crazy Horse up the line along a narrow ridge on Coyote Trail. The wind was up and the storm clouds forecast by Hadley before they set off were already gathering over Whiskey Rock.

'Gee, I'm cold!' Taryn wailed. She sat hunched in Taco's saddle, the sleeves of her sweater pulled way down over her wrists to try and warm her bare hands.

The other kids pressed on into the wind, picking their way along the ridge and trying to ignore a steep drop to their left.

'That Jimmy's a liability!' Kirstie muttered. She watched him barge past Lacey and Squeaky, almost tipping them off the track down the slope. Lacey handled herself well, refusing to panic and reining her horse gently off the trail, yet keeping her balance at an angle of forty-five degrees.

'I like that girl!' Ben breathed, his thin face alert to everything that was going on.

Then, later, as Jimmy came across with an unscheduled, look-at-me lope around the back of Whiskey Rock, the head wrangler once more commented on Lacey's quiet confidence.

'See how she kept Squeaky in check?' he murmured to Kirstie before he galloped off to issue another dire warning to Jimmy. 'And Squeaky's a horse with plenty of juice. It takes a good rider to hold him back when he spots the chance of a race. Do you know anything about the kid?'

Kirstie shook her head. 'Not a lot. Her second name's Darwin. Lives in a place south-west of

Denver. She filled out an application form saying she didn't know how to ride. That's how come she's in the beginners' group.'

'She don't say much.' Ben looked thoughtfully after the untypical guest. Lacey Darwin maintained her good seat; back straight but not stiff, head up, swaying rhymically to the horse's movement.

By now, Lacey was urging Squeaky into a controlled trot, posting nicely in and out of the saddle and ignoring the general hurly-burly of the race to follow Jimmy.

Ben rode off to get the group back together, while Kirstie turned to see Taryn lagging behind.

'I'm c-c-cold!'

Kirstie nodded. 'Didn't you bring a jacket?'

'Nope.'

'So what if it rains?'

'I get wet.' Taryn's bottom lip curled out, spoiling her pretty face. 'Gee, I hate my stupid horse. It won't go where I want it to go, and it won't break out of a lousy walk!'

Taco ain't exactly having a great time either! Kirstie thought. She noted the mare's head hanging, the dejected set of her ears as she plodded along. 'We could turn round and head home early,' she suggested as the first cold drops of rain splashed down.

'You bet!' Jumping at the chance, Taryn jerked on the reins and made Taco flick her head back at the jarring pull of the bit inside her soft mouth.

No sooner said than done. Taryn reined her horse sharply around and pointed back towards the ranch.

So Kirstie yelled a message to Ben, arranging to accompany Taryn. Then they headed down the wooded slope, the wind behind them now, but driving a flurry of hard rain against their backs. Jitterbug skittered sideways in reaction to a distant noise, while Taco kept stolidly on.

'How long?' Taryn grumbled, her hair drenched, her face pinched and blue with cold.

'About an hour.' Kirstie recognised the ridge, and beyond it a stretch of thicker ponderosa pines which might shelter them from the rain.

Then again and again: 'How long?'

'Forty minutes . . . Half an hour.'

Taryn looked like a drowned raccoon, her black mascara smudged and dribbling, her woolly grey sweater clinging to her skinny body. Kirstie herself had donned her yellow slicker and sat dry and warm.

'How long now?'

'Ten minutes.'

They'd reached the valley and rode along the bank of Five Mile Creek. The red roofs of the ranch buildings were in sight.

'J-j-jee-sus, I'm c-c-cold!' Taryn's teeth chattered.

'Give me your horse,' Kirstie offered as they rode by Taryn's cabin. 'You get off here and I'll lead Taco into the corral. I'll take care of her while you take a hot shower.'

Readily agreeing, Taryn dismounted and disappeared. She turned Taco over to Kirstie without a second glance, dived for her cabin porch and disappeared inside.

'No problem!' Kirstie assured the black-and-white mare. Up ahead, through the pouring rain, she could see that Chuck Perry and Hadley had taken refuge in the brand new barn to finish the shoeing. 'It's a nice dry stall for you two, a good feed and a rest!'

'Couldn't take it, huh?' Hadley called out as she rode Jitterbug into the barn and led Taco after them.

'Hah-hah, Hadley. I'm not the one who's been hanging around inside all morning!' Off with the slicker, then off with the two horses' saddles. They

14

blew and snorted, nosed in the empty wooden manger for some sweet alfalfa hay.

There was more banter as everyone went on with their work and the rain beat down on the high iron roof.

'This is a nice little blue roan you have here!' Chuck called out above the clink and ring of hammer against metal shoe. He was bent forward, taking the weight of the horse's fetlock against his knee, rhythmically hammering a nail into Gunsmoke's hoof.

'He's new,' Kirstie replied, heaving a bale of hay from the stack and slicing through the retaining string with a clasp-knife. 'Brad and Ben found him over Mineville way. Place called Bonney Lake.'

'Hey, I know it.' The shoer finished with one hoof and went on to the next. 'I thought I recognised the horse. He belonged to Harry Kohler's girl. Shoed him a couple of times last summer, but I ain't been near for months. Kohler's bad at paying what he owes, so I told him I wouldn't go back this year.'

'That figures.' From what Kirstie knew about Gunsmoke's background, there wasn't a whole lot of care and responsibility around Bonney

Lake. In fact, Ben had told her that the blue roan was in bad condition when he and Brad had put in their offer, and that the family had been glad to be rid of him.

'This little guy's special.' Chuck went on handling the horse with professional ease. 'He's a Paso Fino.'

'Come again!' Kirstie's ears pricked up as she left off feeding Taco and Jitterbug, and went over to listen more closely. 'What's a Paso . . . Fin . . . ?'

'Fino. Special breed. *Los Caballos de Paso Fino*,' the farrier explained without pausing in his work. Each horse took thirty minutes. Any longer, and he was down on his day's earnings. 'It means "the horse with the fine step". The GIs brought them up from Puerto Rico after World War Two. The thing is, they have this real smooth gait, different from a walk, a trot or a lope.'

'The Classic Fino,' Hadley chipped in, not to be outdone by Chuck. 'That's a regular walk, only very fancy and fast forward! Then there's the Paso Corto, like a trot, but real smooth.'

'And the Paso Largo,' Chuck added. *Chink-chink-chink* with the hammer. Gunsmoke shifted slightly and breathed out. 'That's the long stride, something like a lope, but not a lope.'

16

'Hmm.' Kirstie was intrigued.

She liked the look of the horse; especially the swirls of dark and light grey all over his shiny coat. His paler legs were long and straight, his head fine, nostrils wide, and his large eyes were fringed with long, dark lashes.

'He needs plenty of running on him,' Hadley commented, standing back to judge Gunsmoke's deep, broad chest and strong hindquarters. 'Else all this muscle's gonna drop away.'

'Who are you thinking might ride him?' Chuck wanted to know. It was time for him to finish and pack away his tools, drive off along the long dirt road to his next ranch. 'Ain't none of these kids on Kids' Week good enough to work with him, I reckon.'

Hadley didn't disagree. 'It's down to Ben,' he commented. 'He's head wrangler now! All I'm saying is, the horse needs to be worked.'

'You do, don't you?' Kirstie murmured to the blue roan. To her, all horses were special, and a fancy Spanish breed name didn't impress. But she liked Gunsmoke's temperament as well as his looks; he'd been patient and steady while the farrier worked, not quick to spook, and was quiet now as she moved him out of the stall.

And Chuck's throwaway comment rattled around inside her head as Hadley showed the farrier out and she stood in the quiet, dry barn gently stroking the roan's smooth neck. 'Ain't none of these kids good enough to work with him, I reckon . . .'

'The horse needs to be worked . . .'

'No one good enough . . .'

Except maybe one!

Kirstie's grey eyes lit up. Someone who didn't talk much and claimed to be a beginner. A kid with a gentle touch and a natural talent for riding horses.

Lacey Darwin.

Hmm. Kirstie would mention it to Ben, she decided.

Maybe, just maybe, this neat little plan would hatch . . .

2

'Hi there. This is Meredith Kohler. May I speak with Ben Marsh please?'

Kirstie had run into the head wrangler's small office to pick up the phone. It was eight-thirty, Tuesday morning; the sky was blue, Eagle's Peak sharp and clear in the distance.

She put on her polite desk-clerk voice in response to the one at the other end of the phone. 'I'm sorry, Ben is out in the meadow right now. Can I take a message?'

'Sure. You can ask Ben how Gunsmoke is getting along and get him to call me back.'

Gunsmoke – Kohler. Kirstie made the connection between the new blue roan and his previous owners. She felt herself come over a little hostile, recalling the poor state in which Brad and Ben had found the gelding. 'I can tell you that,' she said shortly. 'He's getting along just great, thanks.'

'Yeah?' Meredith obviously wanted to hear more. 'Did he gain weight yet?'

'Yep. From what I hear, Brad Martin kept him at his place just outside San Luis for a couple of weeks. He's got good grazing in the valley there. Then on Saturday he drove Gunsmoke out here in his trailer, along with Little Vixen. We fixed your horse up with a new set of shoes and now he's raring to go.'

'Oh gee, that's cool.' The girl from Bonney Lake sounded surprised yet relieved. 'Y'know the vet, Glen Woodford? He never did find out why that weight dropped off him this summer. He checked his teeth, ran a whole heap of tests, but no way did we get to the bottom of the problem. In the end, Dad reached the point where he said it would be kinder to destroy the horse, put him out of his misery.'

'Well, I'm glad you didn't.' Glancing out of the

small window, Kirstie was able to catch a glimpse of Ben leading the blue roan gelding into the corral right that second. Gunsmoke stepped smoothly across the footbridge from Red Fox Meadow, his marbled blue-grey coat catching the sunlight, his pale grey mane and tail ruffling and swaying as he walked.

'Yeah. Me too. That was when Brad stepped in. He said he thought he could bring the horse round, get the weight back by putting him on a special diet. Ben Marsh saw him too. It was Ben who put in the offer to buy him as a matter of fact, though my dad tried to tell him there was no running left in the horse.'

'Well, it worked out.' Kirstie looked at her watch. She didn't have time to stay and talk. 'Listen, I have to go help in the corral, OK?'

'Wait. You're one hundred per cent sure that Gunsmoke is ready to begin work?'

'Yeah, no problem. You can quit worrying.'

'Hey, and listen. Would it be cool for me to come and see the little guy for myself? I could get someone to drive me out to the ranch later today, maybe.'

By this time Kirstie really had to rush. 'Sure,

why not? I'll mention it to Ben. Better make it about four-thirty.'

'Oh gee, thanks!' Now Meredith sounded excited and pleased. 'See you then.'

'Yeah, see ya.' Kirstie put down the phone and hurried out. *Weird*, she thought. How come Brad and Ben had such a down on the Kohlers? They'd given the impression that Gunsmoke had been badly neglected by the family, yet here was the daughter sounding real concerned and caring. Enough to make the effort to come way out to Half-Moon Ranch and check him out. Kirstie decided that maybe she'd ask Ben about it if she got the time.

But now it was a question of lugging heavy saddles out of the tack-room and getting through the morning routine of tacking up, checking cinches, helping riders into the saddle.

'Thanks, Kirstie.' Cory Shaw grinned down at her from Rodeo Rocky's back. The Texan girl was obviously enjoying every second of her time at the ranch.

'Where's Taryn?' Jimmy Masterson yelled, barging his way towards the gate on Crazy Horse. 'Anybody seen Taryn this morning?'

'Still in bed,' another girl mumbled. 'She don't feel good.'

Ben overheard and gave orders for Charlie, the junior wrangler, to unsaddle Taco and take the mare back to the meadow. Today Ben and Kirstie were to lead the Advanced ride, while Brad went with the beginners. 'Hey, Lacey!' he said to the shy girl who had just walked into the corral, alone as usual. The head wrangler winked across at Kirstie. 'Are you looking for Squeaky by any chance?'

Puzzled, Lacey searched through the rows of horses for her kid-broke bay gelding.

'Squeaky's out in the meadow.' Ben grinned and led her to the far end of the row where Brad was tightening the cinch on Gunsmoke. Then he checked the lead-rope to make sure it was tightly looped around the saddle horn. 'This is your horse for today!'

'Wow!' The girl's pale face, half hidden behind a curtain of straight, dark hair, lit up. Then, just as quickly it shaded over. 'Gee, no, I don't know if I can . . .'

'Sure you can!' Kirstie went across to add her encouragement. 'I saw you ride yesterday. You have a talent, believe me.'

'But I never . . . I mean, this is one cool

horse . . . but I'm only a beginner!'

'Believe me!' Kirstie grinned as she ignored Lacey's protests and helped her into the saddle. 'Compared with some other kids, you really know how to handle yourself.'

'You and Gunsmoke are coming with us today,' Ben informed her. 'The Advanced group is riding out to Dead Man's Canyon through Fat Man's Squeeze. It's tough territory, but Gunsmoke is a real smooth ride. You'll do just fine.'

'Yeah, great!' Jimmy grunted as he overheard. He refused to shift Crazy Horse so that Lacey and Gunsmoke could ride by. 'How come she gets the best horse on the whole ranch?'

'Take no notice,' Kirstie murmured as Lacey hesitated and blushed. Quickly she mounted Lucky and led the shy guest to join Ben. The Advanced ride was ready to leave. 'All the horses at Half-Moon Ranch are top quarter-horses,' she told Jimmy. 'Grade A. It's some of the riders who ain't too hot!'

The mountains soon made them forget the niggles and awkwardness of the corral.

They rose out of the belt of dark pine trees, ruggedly overlapping into the far blue distance.

The jagged horizon seemed to roll on forever, while underfoot the horses' tread was muffled by an endless carpet of fallen aspen leaves, the ground dappled yellow and gold, orange and brilliant scarlet.

'Bushwhack!' At Dead Man's Canyon, Ben gave the order for the group to split away from the nose-to-tail line and pick their own way up to Fat Man's Squeeze.

'Great!' Cory and Rocky broke into a lope between the slender silver trunks of the stand of aspens.

But Kirstie noticed Lacey hold Gunsmoke back.

'It's OK. It looks kinda steep and scary, but you'll be fine,' she told her. 'Trust your horse, let him pick his own route. All you have to do is go with the flow.'

Nodding, Lacey relaxed Gunsmoke's reins and clicked him from walk to trot.

'No need to post the trot.' Kirstie and Lucky kept pace. 'Gunsmoke has this special gait which Hadley and Chuck Perry told me about. There's no jolt in the stride. I notice when he's at walking speed it looks real fancy but it comes out without jarring one little bit. Now he's trotting – they call it the Paso Corto – he's still one hundred per cent smooth . . .'

'Yeah, I could ride him all day!' Lacey let herself go and slid into the rhythm of the Paso Fino's easy movement. She wove in and out of the trees, leaning sideways to avoid low branches, then slightly forward in the saddle to ease the horse's climb up the steep gradient towards two overhanging rocks.

And Kirstie saw how willingly Gunsmoke went. Only a little over fourteen hands high, the roan gelding looked at the same time neat and dainty, yet strong. And he was a classy guy. His large nostrils and small muzzle gave him the appearance of good breeding, together with the wide-set eyes. His back was short, his chest deep.

'What did you pay for Gunsmoke?' Watching Lacey make good progress, Kirstie hung back to chat with Ben.

The wrangler narrowed his eyes and pretended to look suspicious. 'Who wants to know?'

'I do. I'd say I was looking at a couple of thousand dollars' worth of horse up there!'

'Hah!' Ben was riding Matt's horse, Cadillac, while Kirstie's brother spent the day at college. He urged the big thoroughbred into a trot and curved around a large boulder, scaring a ground squirrel into whisking its tail and scurrying out of sight under a log. 'The horse was only fit for dogmeat when Brad and me found him. I offered Harry Kohler a couple of *hundred* to take him off his hands.'

'That was a good deal!' Kirstie admired the flow of Gunsmoke's unusual gait. 'But didn't you take a risk all the same? From what I hear, the horse had a feeding problem that looked like it could be fatal.'

'Feeding problem . . . yeah!' The normally laid-back Ben curled his lip in scorn. 'The only problem Gunsmoke had with his feed was that the Kohlers weren't giving him none!'

'But I spoke with Meredith!'

'You did? When?'

'This morning. Sorry, I forgot to tell you. She's fixed to pay Gunsmoke a visit this afternoon. She said they'd run a hundred tests with Glen Woodford to check the horse out. She sounded real relieved that he got better.'

'Yeah!' Ben said a second time. He screwed his bony face into a tight frown as he observed Lacey and Gunsmoke negotiate the dark, narrow alley of Fat Man's Squeeze with quiet confidence. 'Don't ask me just what's going on here, but I can tell you one thing for sure: the Kohlers never took that gelding anywhere near no vet!'

'So how was that?' Kirstie asked Lacey as they rode home by Five Mile Creek. She could tell by the guest's face what the answer would be.

'Did I die and go to heaven?' Lacey breathed. Her brown eyes beneath the peak of her faded denim cap were alive with the wonder of the mountain ride. She and Gunsmoke trotted along the level valley bottom as one.

'You certain you never rode before you came here?' Kirstie quizzed.

'Never,' Lacey assured her. 'No, I tell a lie. I rode a pony at my gran's place in New Jersey – before – well, a long time ago. I was five years old. I guess.'

Kirstie smiled at Lucky's attempt to alter his gait to fit in alongside the odd rhythm of the Paso Fino. The palomino tried to achieve something between a walk and a trot, but stumbled and grew confused. He shook his blond mane, snorted, then reverted to an extended walk. 'And how old are you now?'

'Thirteen.'

Kirstie nodded. They rode for a while in

silence. 'So, if you don't ride, how come you visited Half-Moon Ranch?'

Lacey shrugged. 'It was my mom's idea. She thought it would help . . .' Once more, the girl's conversation faded. Then she glanced sideways at Kirstie and decided to plunge on. 'My mom just remarried,' she told her. 'Steve, my new dad, and I don't get along too good.'

'Yeah.' Kirstie didn't try to fill the next silence. She'd had plenty of *that* thank you. She recalled the split between her own mom and dad four years earlier, the move out to the ranch with Sandy, the heartache. 'You live near Denver?' she asked quietly, without getting a reply. 'So where's your real dad?'

'He died when I was seven. Mom and I were OK after a year or two. But now Steve has to come along . . .'

Kirstie sighed and nodded. 'So maybe things will be better when you get back home?'

Another shrug, the same fading, empty voice. 'I doubt it.'

'So anyway, you had a good day today?' Kirstie wanted to end on an up-note as the ranch drew near.

She got a brief smile from Lacey before the

visitor slid into a lope along the side of the creek. 'Yeah, cool!' she murmured.

Her long, dark hair flew straight back; the spray from the stream flew up like bright gems from under Gunsmoke's newly-shod hooves.

'Yeah, you died and went to heaven!' Kirstie murmured sadly. A problem like Lacey's was a problem she was glad she didn't have.

'Hey, Lacey, you were cool!' Back in the corral, Cory let everyone know about the shy girl's success on Gunsmoke. The cheerful Texan unsaddled Rocky then cosied up alongside her tough ex-rodeo mount.

Rocky nuzzled Cory's hand for a reward in the shape of candy.

'Everyone, Lacey here is an excellent rider!'

'Cory, hush up!' Lacey protested. She hid her face behind her hair as she brushed Gunsmoke's dappled coat.

'Yeah, yeah!' Just back from his own trail-ride, Jimmy swung from the saddle and let his tired horse wander away. 'Little Miss Perfect Rider! – with a little help from a docile dummy of a horse!' He sneered in Taryn's direction as he noticed the day's non-rider slouch towards the fence.

'Yeah, that's a Mickey Mouse pony you got yourself there, Lacey. Gunsmoke's about as full of life as a painted carousel horse!' Taryn's drawl drew an approving yelp from Jimmy. The two went off together to find Brad and make life difficult for him instead.

'You gonna teach me one of those sliding stops?' Jimmy demanded as he spotted Brad working with Little Vixen in the arena.

'Sure, if you wanna break your neck!' was Brad's sarcastic reply.

'What did I do to Jimmy and Taryn?' Lacey breathed. She had to swallow hard and bite her lip to stop it from trembling.

'Zilch. Pay them no mind.' Kirstie set to with curry comb and brush while Lucky kept a wary eye on Gunsmoke. The palomino was still trying to decide exactly where the freakish roan should fit into the pecking order on the ranch.

'I didn't ask to be moved into Advanced.' Unable to let the subject drop, Lacey struggled to control her feelings as she worked on.

'I know that. Ben knows that. Why let them bug you?'

'That's easy to say. But hey, you're not the one they'll whisper about behind your back. You're not the one they ignore at supper. They don't steal your riding boots and hide them in the laundry.'

'They did that?' Kirstie frowned.

'Yeah. That was Saturday. Sunday, they took the boots and dumped them in the hot-tub.' A tear had spilled on to Lacey's cheek in spite of her efforts to stop it. She wiped it away quickly with the cuff of her jacket.

'Gee, that's so juuvenile!'

'Uh-huh. I wish I knew what I did to make them dislike me.' Lacey had taken the humiliations on board and seemed helpless to do anything about it.

Kirstie was angry on her behalf. There was nothing about Lacey that drew the bullies and made her their victim, except perhaps her unusual shyness. 'Forget it,' she advised. But like Lacey said, that was easier said than done.

Luckily, it was right then that Meredith Kohler fulfilled her promise to come and visit Gunsmoke.

Kirstie noticed a sleek red sports car drive under the entrance to the ranch and down the last stretch of dirt track into the yard. She hurried to the fence, ducked and was almost under the top rung when she remembered to call back an instruction to Lacey not to take the blue roan down to the ford by the bridge and let him loose into the meadow. 'He has a visitor!' she yelled. 'Scrub him up good, ready to meet his ex-owner!'

By this time, a woman and her daughter had stepped out of the car. Kirstie could tell they were related by their similar round faces and high cheekbones, not to mention the fancy western wear they both had on.

Meredith especially was keen to strut her stuff. She wore her wavy blonde hair loose, the collar of her white-and-black leather jacket turned up. The short jacket was heavily studded and fringed, the girl's black denim jeans clasped tight at the waist by a belt with a big silver buckle. Mrs Kohler's outfit was similar, except that her hair was pinned high and she wore more cosmetics to emphasise her columbine-blue eyes.

Kirstie noticed that Charlie and Hadley had both sauntered out of the tack-room and leaned on the rail to catch an eyeful of the new arrivals.

'Hey, I'm Kirstie Scott.' She hurried across the yard, determined not to be dazzled by the glamour. 'You must be Meredith!'

The girl, who was about Kirstie's own age but who looked twice as sophisticated, treated her to a brilliant white smile. 'How's Gunsmoke? How's my little guy?'

She faltered under the bright gaze. Meredith had eyes as blue as her mother's and they exuded confidence. The look from them seemed to highlight Kirstie's own down-home checked cotton shirt and faded jeans. 'Come and see for yourself,' she suggested, eager to turn around and get this over with.

'Oh, there he is!' Meredith spotted Gunsmoke in the corral and took off at a graceful, long-legged run.

Letting her pass, Kirstie waited for the mother, who sighed with pleasure and took her time to cross the yard.

'Gee, it's a pity!' Mrs Kohler murmured, turquoise earrings dangling against the collar of her jacket.

Kirstie didn't get it. 'How come?'

'It's a shame we had to let Gunsmoke go.'

Together they stopped and watched Meredith rush to fling her arms around the lovely little Paso Fino's neck. Gunsmoke recognised her at once and pricked his ears and stamped one foot.

'See!' The girl's mother seemed overcome with emotion. She took a deep breath and shook her head. 'My baby just loves that horse. Always did! Always will!'

3

'Kirstie, did you ask Meredith and Mrs Kohler to stay for the barn dance tonight?' Charlie dropped in the question as he strolled across the corral.

Word about the glamorous visitors had got round fast. It seemed that they had made a strong impression.

'No!' Kirstie hissed back at the young wrangler. She noticed Lacey standing uncomfortably to one side as Meredith went on fussing and petting Gunsmoke. The dark-haired girl looked more alone and left-out than ever.

'You're welcome to come along, Mrs Kohler.

It's no big deal; a couple of people knock out a tune on guitars while the rest of us get to hoe-down.' Charlie pressed on regardless, giving Meredith's mother the encouragement she needed. Then he offered to introduce her to Sandy Scott.

As they walked off together towards the house, Kirstie made up her mind to check a few things out with the daughter. 'So Gunsmoke looks good, huh?' she said casually, leaning on the fence, hands clasped, with one foot balanced on the bottom rung.

'Yeah, he's my gorgeous guy!' Meredith cooed some more, then tried to rub the gelding's muzzle with the flat of her hand.

Gunsmoke jerked his head back and flattened his ears. Tethered to the rail, he shifted his rear end sideways, so that Lacey had to step quickly out of his way.

'Yeah. The weird thing is, Brad never mentioned a feeding problem when he took care of him. He just had to bulk him up with good quality alfalfa. And Ben, our head wrangler, got Glen Woodford to check him over, bring his medical history up-to-date with repeat jabs . . . y'know.' Kirstie was deliberately laid-back, but still she detected a slight prickle in the visitor's reaction at the mention of the vet's name.

'I guess the problem sorted itself out,' Meredith suggested, fondling Gunsmoke's long, supple neck. 'Maybe he had an allergy to the pasture at Bonney Lake. That would clear up as soon as he left our place.'

'Yeah.' Ducking under the fence, Kirstie went to join the small group. She noted that the blue roan was uneasy with the attention he was getting and suggested to Lacey that she untie him, ready to lead him out to the meadow.

'Oh no, hold it!' Meredith pleaded, circling her arms around the reluctant horse's neck. 'I came all this way to see my guy. Just give me a little more time!'

Kirstie nodded. 'So Glen was the vet you hired at Bonney Lake?'

'Yeah . . . well, maybe no!' Meredith smiled her way out of a tight corner. 'I guess my dad used someone else. Did I say Glen Woodford to you when we spoke on the phone?'

'You did.' Kirstie's eyes narrowed as she bent to pick up Gunsmoke's front foot and examine his new shoe. 'Only, Brad said that couldn't be right, because Glen had no records for the horse.'

'I screwed up,' Meredith admitted. 'But hey, I don't get involved. It's my dad who pays the bills and takes care of that side of things.'

Grunting, Kirstie lowered Gunsmoke's hoof. 'So we have a mystery.'

'Hey, listen . . . !' Meredith objected, the smile suddenly vanishing.

'No, not about the vet. I mean, a mystery about why Gunsmoke wouldn't eat,' Kirstie cut in. She saw her mom come out of the house on to the porch with Charlie and Mrs Kohler. 'But the great thing is, he's in good shape now.'

Meredith too saw her mother and ran daintily to the corral fence. 'Mom, did you see how pleased Gunsmoke was to see me? Doesn't he look cool? He's totally recovered and as gorgeous as ever!'

Mrs Kohler smiled indulgently as she swished across the yard with Sandy and Charlie, the long fringes on her jacket swinging. 'Yeah. I was explaining to these good folks how much the horse means to you. I told them it broke your heart when you had to part with him.'

Like, yeah! Kirstie thought darkly. She imagined, perhaps a touch unkindly, that Meredith Kohler was more likely to break her heart over a chipped fingernail than the loss of a horse. Taking a glance in Lacey Darwin's direction, she saw that she had an ally in her low opinion of the fancy visitor.

'All this is making me feel kinda bad,' Sandy confessed. 'I had no idea how Meredith felt about Gunsmoke. I guess I imagined he'd been pretty unloved and unwanted to have gotten in such poor condition.'

'I can see why you thought that,' Mrs Kohler murmured. She gave a loud sigh as she gazed at her daughter and the roan horse. 'But you see, nothing could be further from the truth.'

'So I'm wondering what we can do about it.' Thoughtfully Sandy ducked under the fence to inspect the Paso Fino. 'It's like I almost stole the horse, paying a couple of hundred bucks when he's obviously worth so much more.'

A deal's a deal! Kirstie thought. She could see her mom was softening rapidly under the guilt trip that was being laid on her.

'The dough's not the issue,' Mrs Kohler said, giving the same bright but empty smile as her daughter. 'It's just that Meredith misses Gunsmoke so!'

They want him back! Kirstie saw the truth with

sudden, startling clarity. *The Kohlers heard he recovered his health and so he's worth a whole lot more than they sold him for. Yet they're too mean to buy him back. They just want to soft-soap us and get him back for nothing, then sell him to the highest bidder. That's why they're here!*

'I understand.' Sandy nodded, running her hand lightly along the gelding's strong back. 'He's a great horse,' she agreed. 'Say, let me think about this, will you?'

'Sure!' Mrs Kohler knew when not to push her luck. 'Meredith, honey; Charlie invited us to the dance tonight, so we're gonna stick around.'

'Lacey, you can take Gunsmoke out to Red Fox Meadow now,' Kirstie's mom said quietly, still deep in thought.

Kirstie too knew that it was time to let Lucky go eat. Together they slipped the knots on the halter ropes and walked the two horses down to the creek.

'Call me suspicious,' Kirstie muttered, unbuckling the palomino's headcollar at the water's edge. 'But I don't reckon Meredith Kohler gives a damn about her ex-horse!'

Her remark dropped into the evening stillness. She watched Lucky lower his head to drink, then step calmly across the stream.

Meanwhile, Lacey softly stroked Gunsmoke's cheek before she unfastened his headcollar. The horse turned his head to nuzzle her hand. Then he followed Lucky's lead and began to drink.

Lacey stepped back up the sandy bank. She cleared her throat to speak, hesitated, then delivered her verdict on the puzzle surrounding the Kohlers. 'It isn't Meredith I care about,' she said, slow and deliberate.

She watched the blue roan step steadily into the creek, the gleaming water swirling round his knees until he pulled himself up the far bank. Then he threw back his head and broke the silence with a shrill whinny. Lucky turned to wait. The Paso Fino broke into his peculiar smooth gait, circled the palomino, then drew close. Then the two horses put their heads peaceably together to graze.

'So if it's not Meredith, what is it?' Kirstie asked.

Lacey delivered her verdict. 'The thing that really bugs me concerns Gunsmoke and the way he acted when Meredith was around. Did you see his ears?'

'Yeah. They laid right back against his neck.'

'And he didn't want her to touch his muzzle.

He was expecting a slap, not a stroke.'

True. Kirstie realised that Lacey had hit the nail on the head.

'This horse does not like Meredith Kohler!' she declared. 'Whatever the family tells us, I reckon that no way did the Kohlers treat him right!'

'Yee-hah!' Jimmy Masterson yelled and swung Taryn round and round.

Two lines of dancers clapped and tapped their feet as the noisy lead couple sidestepped down the middle.

'Couple number two take up the lead!' Hadley called.

'That's us!' Meredith Kohler shrieked at Charlie, who grabbed her round the waist and swung her. Her blonde hair flew back, her heeled boots clicked on the wooden floor, then the wrangler sidestepped her between the lines.

'Couple number three!' Hadley cried. Between calling, he blew into his harmonica to produce a rapid, rhythmical tune.

Matt Scott played guitar from his seat by the stone fireplace, his girlfriend, Lachelle, standing close by.

Number three couple was Cory Shaw and Ben

Marsh. Kirstie would be next after that with Brad Martin. Brad would swing her clean off her feet, whooping and hollering with the best.

'Yee-hah!' Ben and Cory swung and moved smoothly on.

'Ready?' Brad grinned.

'Ready!' Kirstie leaned her weight away from him. They started to spin.

'Yeah, go Brad! Go Kirstie!' the others yelled.

Her head whirled; her feet left the ground. She yelled and laughed, breathless as Brad swept her down the line.

And on, weaving circles and figures of eight, crashing together in clumsy dosi-dos, people laughing and falling about, kids going crazy to the lively music as Matt moved on into a tune called the Salty Dog Rag and Hadley yelled out instructions for the new steps.

'Enough!' Kirstie gasped at Brad. 'Go ask Mom to dance instead!'

'You bet!' He dropped her hand in a flash and wove between the other dancers to find Sandy, leaving her to draw breath.

But then Kirstie saw Lacey standing out of the new dance. That was no good; everyone should be joining in. The problem was, there weren't enough men to go around. There was only one solution. Kirstie dashed over and pulled Lacey on to the floor. 'I'll be the guy, you be the gal!' she grinned.

Blushing, Lacey struggled, then gave in. She stood with Kirstie and watched Meredith and Charlie demonstrate the steps to Salty Dog Rag.

The teaching over, Hadley called for everyone to try it out and set the music in full swing. Couples criss-crossed the room, stepping and turning in time.

'Hey, look at Meredith and Charlie go!' Sandy pointed out the best dancers on the floor. She was having a good time partnering Brad, relaxing as everyone enjoyed themselves after a hard day's riding.

'Wouldn't you just know Meredith would be a great dancer!' Kirstie muttered. She tried to steer Lacey between Jimmy and Taryn and another couple, but the gap was too tight and they all crashed.

'Jesus!' Taryn complained, hopping on one foot. Then she passed a remark about Lacey and Kirstie under her breath which made Jimmy burst out in raucous laughter.

'Yeah!' he croaked. 'Right on, Taryn! C'mon,

let's get out of here before we break a leg!'

Kirstie watched him drag his girl off while Lacey's face turned bright red.

'I'll sit out, I guess,' the introverted and sensitive girl whispered, blundering away in confusion over Taryn's sneaky insult.

Kirstie frowned then sighed, but she let Lacey slide away. *If it was down to me, I wouldn't let them get to me!* she told herself. *Sticks and stones may break my bones* . . . Lacey needed an extra layer of skin to get her through life, she decided, shaking her head sadly and wandering off to find a cold drink.

'. . . Yeah, and you know something?' Taryn was still sniggering and giggling with Jimmy over by the drink dispenser. She didn't see Kirstie's approach. 'Besides the fact that Lacey Darwin has two left feet and can't get a guy to ask her to dance, she sneaks her way out of the Beginners' group and on to the best-looking horse on the entire ranch just by putting on that lonely "Poor me" act!'

'Right on!' Jimmy agreed. Over his shoulder he must have spotted Lacey hovering beside the door. And he surely knew that she'd overheard Taryn's latest cutting remark. But instead of warning his girlfriend to cut it out, he decided to encourage her. 'What makes Lacey Darwin so special?'

'Nothing!' Taryn had it in for Lacey big-time. Maybe she was jealous of her natural riding talent. Or maybe Lacey's quiet way of keeping herself to herself unsettled someone so loud and upfront as Taryn. 'One big fat zero. Lacey might think she's different from the rest of us, but believe me, the only special thing about her is her cry-baby attitude!'

Kirstie stepped up to the drinks table too late to stop Jimmy and Taryn shredding Lacey's reputation. She saw Lacey's stricken look and watched helplessly as the poor kid faded backwards through the door. 'Cool!' she snapped sarcastically, gesturing in the direction of the empty doorway. 'I hope you're happy!'

'Huh?' Jimmy pretended not to understand.

'Oh . . . go boil your head!' *Childish? Yes. Useful? No.*

Taryn and Jimmy burst into loud laughter as Kirstie stormed away.

'So you'll think through what we talked about?' Mrs Kohler was saying to Sandy Scott outside the ranch house under a starlit sky.

The visitor had dragged Meredith away early from the barn dance in order to make the drive back to Bonney Lake. Now she and her daughter were having a final word with the boss of Half-Moon Ranch.

Kirstie had come across them as she went out to search for Lacey, and she paused to catch her mom's reply over the faint sound of music still continuing in the large dining room.

'I'll give it some thought,' Sandy agreed.

'It would make Meredith very happy.' Mrs Kohler impressed on the ranch owner how much the issue of Gunsmoke meant to her daughter. 'Of course, we'll understand if you decide to keep the horse. After all, you did buy him fair and square.'

Meredith had turned her big blue eyes on Sandy and was imploring silently.

Yeah, they want him back! Kirstie repeated her earlier conviction. *And I bet it's for two hundred measly dollars, even after we took care of him, paid the vet and got him back into good shape!*

'Like I said, I'll consider it. Let me talk to Ben.' Sandy held out under the pressure of Meredith's pleading look. 'I'll call you tomorrow.'

So the two women shook hands and Kirstie made a resolution to communicate her suspicions about the Kohlers to her mom. She would point out the risk of sending Gunsmoke back to a place where he seemed to have been badly treated. She would pass on Lacey's belief that the horse was afraid of his ex-owners.

But for now she had to concentrate on finding Lacey and telling her one more time that no way were Taryn and Jimmy worth losing sleep over.

This could prove difficult, she realised, as she gazed out beyond the corral towards the guest cabins spread out on the hillside. First, she would check Lacey's cabin; the most obvious place. After that, maybe the barn.

I only hope she didn't go walkabout! she said to herself, leaving her mom to see off the Kohlers. Being a city kid, Lacey might not know that wildcats, coyotes and even bears roamed the foothills of the Meltwater Range at night. Anyways, it wasn't a good idea to wander near any sheer drops, even when the moon was shining and the stars were out.

Kirstie's feet crunched up the track to Trail's End Cabin. *Taryn and Jimmy suck!* she thought grimly, wondering if the pair would still treat

Lacey the way they did if they knew the problems she had at home. *Yeah, they probably would*, she told herself. The juvenile tricks with the boots, the sneaky remarks were just part of the way they were; period.

And when they saw that they could get under Lacey's thin skin, it only made them worse.

There was no light on in the cabin, and no reply to Kirstie's knock. She retraced her steps, lost in thought, and when she reached the corral again a vague notion took hold of her to go and look at the horses in the ramuda.

This is the place I come when I feel bad, she reminded herself, crossing the footbridge with echoing steps. The creek swirled and gurgled by, the black water gleaming silver from the light of the moon. *If I want to be peaceful, there's nothing like being with horses and breathing in the cool, clear night*.

And sure enough, there was a solitary figure by the gate of the meadow.

Lacey stood gazing down the valley, caught in a spell of silence. The horses moved like shadows, stopped to crop the grass, moved on again into blackness.

Kirstie came close without speaking. She

searched for the right phrase; something that would heal the wound of Taryn and Jimmy's callous disregard of Lacey's feelings.

But before she had time to find it, her presence broke through the shell of the girl's isolation and cracked what little remained of her self-possession.

'Go away – please!' Lacey whispered in a faltering, broken voice.

'I want to help.'

'You can't. Nobody can.' A sob rose from her chest as she turned away and began to stumble through the long grass, deeper into the night.

'Lacey . . . !'

'Go away! Why won't you leave me alone?' A desperate, fading cry as she ran on.

And Kirstie had to let her go. Because there was nothing you could say to someone who was as unhappy as this. No words of comfort. No sticking plaster you could possibly put over the wound.

4

'It takes a little patience,' Brad explained to Lacey early next morning.

Yawning and still half asleep, Kirstie could hear the conversation from inside the barn where she was cleaning tack ready for the day's trail-rides. Charlie was whistling the Salty Dog Rag as he too sorted out bits and bridles.

'Learning how to rein ain't something that comes today or tomorrow. I spent years practising in the yard when I was a kid. You get the balance right first, then the pressure from your legs and heels . . .'

A scrunch of gravel told Kirstie and Charlie that he was demonstrating the sliding stop.

'What's going on?' Strolling to the door, Charlie poked out his head. 'Hey, since when did Brad become Lacey Darwin's personal trainer?'

'Don't ask me.' Kirstie assured him that she knew nothing about the lesson taking place in the arena. In fact, the last time she'd seen Lacey had been in the meadow the night before. She'd spent a restless night thinking about the kid's problems, and the last thing she'd expected was to find Lacey up bright and early, taking a lesson from Brad Martin. So she stood up, stretched, then went to stand beside Charlie.

The light outside was still pale grey, and a dawn mist clung to the peaks on the horizon. Two blue jays on the tack-room roof scuttled and hopped along the ridge, then flapped their wings and flew heavily across the creek towards the meadow. Wrapped up in a high-necked sweater and warm blue jacket, wearing her familiar denim cap, Lacey sat in the saddle waiting for Brad to issue his next instruction.

'You ready to try again?' the expert asked. Noticing that they had an unexpected audience, he called out to Charlie and Kirstie. 'Hey, guys!

Get a load of this fancy rider on the blue roan.'

A bashful Lacey shrank away, turning her head and reining her horse to the far side of the arena.

'OK, concentrate. I want you to ride Gunsmoke hard around the arena a couple of times, then turn him fast so that he cuts right across the middle. Got that?'

Lacy nodded and built herself up, ready to begin.

'By about the middle of the arena, you gotta shift your weight way back and rein him in real tight. His front legs will brace and the back ones come under him, like he's trying to sit. At that point, you throw your weight forward, keeping the rein real tight. Got it?'

'What if I don't lean forward at the right time?' Lacey's breath came short as her nerves got the better of her.

'Then you and the horse crash right through the fence and end up in Ben and Charlie's bunkhouse!' Brad grinned. 'Listen, you can do this, no problem!'

'I can?'

'Yeah. I've seen the way you ride. So c'mon, let's go!'

Kirstie saw Lacey take a deep breath then kick

Gunsmoke into action around the rim of the arena. Horse and rider built up speed from walk to trot, then into an easy lope.

'It's lookin' good!' Brad encouraged.

'That kid's a natural!' Charlie muttered, impressed by Lacey's control of Gunsmoke. 'She looks like she's part of the horse.'

'Yeah well, tell her.' After last night's barn dance fiasco, Kirstie badly wanted people to build Lacey's confidence during her last few days at the ranch. 'She needs to know.'

Once, twice around the circle, Gunsmoke loped with his smooth stride. His head was up, ears alert, enjoying every second of the exercise.

'Now turn across the diameter!' Brad called.

Lacey reined the horse to the left by laying the right rein against his neck. He swerved sharply and altered his course to head directly towards the spot where Kirstie and Charlie stood.

'Oh my!' Kirstie breathed.

Gunsmoke was still going at full gallop, Lacey's knees were braced, her loose hair whipped back from her face, which was tense. Her hand gripped the rein and she eased him in.

'Throw your weight back now!' Brad yelled.

Lacey sat down hard and did as she was told.

The action brought the horse's back legs sliding under him while his front legs stayed straight and braced.

'And forward!' Brad cried.

Lacey leaned her weight towards the horse's head. His hooves raised yellow dust as they scrunched and slid for a distance of twenty feet.

'Wow!' Charlie muttered. He set up loud applause, which Kirstie joined in.

Gunsmoke had finally come to a halt five feet from the fence.

'Right on!' Brad whooped. He dropped down from Little Vixen's back and ran to congratulate his student. 'What did I tell you? This stuff is no problem to you.'

As the dust rose then cleared, Lacey's face became visible once more. All the tension was gone, replaced by a broad grin. 'Did I do it?' she asked.

'Did you do it?' the trainer echoed. 'I'd give you full marks if I was a judge in a reining contest!'

'Really?' The grin spread as Lacey leaned forward to reward her horse with a hearty pat on the neck.

Brad took hold of Gunsmoke's reins and nodded proudly. 'Really and truly. Man, I know what I'm saying. And so do Kirstie and Charlie. What d'you think?'

'Cool!' Charlie confirmed.

Great start to the day, Kirstie thought. Terrific idea for the reining expert to pick Lacey out from amongst all the kids in the group and make her feel special. She made a note to pass on to Matt what a good guy their mom's new boyfriend really was.

And Brad led the blue roan back to the start, ready for Lacey to begin again. 'Man, you look like you were born in the saddle!' he told her. 'Here comes Ben, crawling out of the bunkhouse still half asleep. How about we wake him up by showing him exactly what you and Gunsmoke can do?'

'Kirstie, do you think that maybe you're confusing the issue here?' Sandy Scott had listened to her daughter's arguments for not sending Gunsmoke back to Bonney Lake. It was Wednesday evening; the end of another good day out on the trails.

'How come?' Kirstie had put the case against the Kohlers as plain as could be. Number one: whatever the reason, Gunsmoke had definitely suffered under their care. Number two: Kirstie didn't trust either the mother or the daughter. She was convinced that they only wanted the horse back at the original low price so they could sell him on for a bigger profit.

'Haven't you got reason all mixed up with feelings? Ain't it that you've fallen in love with the little guy like you usually do and you're inventing excuses not to send him back to Bonney Lake?'

'No way!' Kirstie wished her mom would give her more credit. 'If you don't believe me, ask Brad and Ben!'

Luckily for her, the two guys were sitting on the bunkhouse porch swing, feet up on the rail. She coaxed Sandy across to get them to add weight to her own opinion.

'Should Mom send Gunsmoke back to the Kohlers?' she demanded right out.

'Nope.' Brad didn't hesitate. To him it was as clear as day. He didn't even stop the gently swinging motion of the wooden seat to think it through.

Sandy frowned and turned to her head wrangler.

'Why would you wanna do that?' Ben queried.

'Because I feel bad!' Sandy explained.

'Meredith and her mom made all that effort to drive over yesterday. It shows how much they care about the horse!'

'No it doesn't!' Kirstie argued hotly. She knew she should try to be cool and reasonable, but she was swept along nevertheless. 'All they care about is dollar signs – ker-ching!'

'How do you know that?' Sandy's troubled expression ranged across the yard to where Lacey and Gunsmoke were practising reining techniques in the arena.

'I don't know for sure, but I got the feeling that she's right.' Ben's quiet manner was a good balance to Kirstie's impassioned plea. 'Anyways, I had my own suspicions last night when they showed up, so today I made it my business to call Glen Woodford in San Luis and check out the sob story about the horse falling sick at Bonney Lake.'

Kirstie's eyes sparkled. 'And?'

'And one thing's for sure: no vet went near Gunsmoke while the Kohlers had him. They were too mean to pay anyone to take care of the horse. Glen stopped going when they refused to pay his bills.'

'Like Chuck Perry!' Kirstie recalled a similar story from the shoer.

'Yeah. And Glen knows for a fact that every other vet in this part of Colorado had the same experience. Besides, he ran some blood tests and he has records to prove that Gunsmoke had no jabs to protect him from disease and that his poor condition was down to plain starvation and general bad treatment!'

'You see!' Kirstie turned eagerly to her mom. 'Now do you believe me?'

'But how come the Kohlers put on such a sneaky act?' Sandy murmured, then sighed. 'No, don't answer that. The real question is, how come I'm such a sucker I believed them?'

Brad stood up from the swing and put an arm loosely around her shoulder. 'Because you're a nice person, Sandy Scott; not a mean person. That's why we like you!'

Kirstie watched her mom smile faintly and allow herself to be led off towards the ranch house for supper. 'So Gunsmoke gets to stay at Half-Moon Ranch?' she called after them.

'Yeah, he does,' Sandy replied over her shoulder. 'I'll call the Kohlers first thing tomorrow and tell them it's no deal!'

So Kirstie went around on Cloud Nine. 'You get

to stay!' she told Gunsmoke as she led him out to the meadow. 'You hear that, Lucky; Gunsmoke here is a fully signed-up member of the Half-Moon ramuda!'

Her palomino's curiosity about the Paso Fino had brought him over from a manager full of best hay. He gave the newcomer's pale grey mane a friendly nibble then invited him to join the feast.

'Gunsmoke's staying!' Kirstie passed on the good news to Charlie, then to Hadley.

'Good job!' The old man's congratulation was worth having. He never praised without meaning it. 'Your mom had me worried back there. The blue roan is the best trail-riding horse Ben bought since he took over!'

With Hadley's seal of approval ringing in her ears, Kirstie went to join the group of guests for an evening cook-out by the creek. Late for the meal of barbecued steak, she took a plate loaded down with food then went off in search of Lacey Darwin.

'You seen Lacey?' she asked Cory Shaw.

'Down by the footbridge,' the Texan girl replied.

'Hmm.' Kirstie spotted a small knot of kids including Lacey, Jimmy and Taryn, all fooling around by the water. Unless Jimmy and Taryn had just had personality transplants, the situation looked like trouble.

And she was right. The two had already ganged up on Lacey and were urging three others to join in.

'Grab the other one!' Jimmy yelled to a boy called Hans, holding one of Lacey's boots aloft.

Lacey hopped on one foot, trying to fend Hans off.

'C'mon, where's your sense of humour, you guys?' Taryn called. 'Lacey don't mind, do you, Lace?' Her face had a sneaky, superior smile which turned defiant the moment she saw Kirstie.

'Shall I? . . . Shall I?' Jimmy crowed. He ran on to the bridge and held the boot above the creek like a trophy, then threatened to let it drop. 'Oops . . . almost!'

'Hey, that's not funny!' Cory had followed Kirstie down to the creek and now set up a protest. 'Leave her alone, why don't you?'

By this time, Lacey had overbalanced and slid down the bank half into the water. She was silent and pale, her face showing an agony of humiliation.

'Aw, c'mon!' Taryn pushed Hans aside and

made out as if to offer Lacey a hand to haul her up the bank. But she deliberately let her slip back, so that Lacey ended up knee-deep in the creek. A hoot of laughter followed from Jimmy on the bridge.

Grim-faced, Kirstie set down her plate and ran to help. Out of the corner of her eye, she was glad to catch sight of her mom striding quickly towards them to find out what was going on. 'Give me your hand!' she called to Lacey, her heart melting at the poor kid's stricken look.

Up on the bridge, Jimmy pushed the joke as far as it would go. 'Oops!' he cried again. This time he actually let go of Lacey's boot and watched it splash into the creek. 'Oh gee, look at that! It floats!'

'It floats like a boat!' Taryn laughed. She had no idea that Sandy Scott was drawing near. 'Lacey's boot is a boat, hah-hah!'

But as Kirstie and Cory both helped Lacey out of the water, Hans and the two others in the gang dropped their uneasy smiles and went quiet. They stood back to let the boss of the ranch through.

'Taryn, you fetch that boot right now,' Sandy instructed quietly.

'No way; I'll get my feet wet!'

'You fetch it,' Kirstie's mom repeated.

Screwing up her face, Lacey's tormentor waded into the creek to pick up the boot.

'And Jimmy, I hold you and Taryn responsible.'

'Hey, no way! We're on vacation. Can't we kid around if we feel like it?' Jimmy stuck his hands in his pockets, came down from the bridge and made as if to stroll away from the scene.

Sandy stepped quickly in front of him, her eyes steely, her voice deceptively even. Behind the coolness, Kirstie recognised real anger. 'I don't find your actions acceptable, Jimmy. I plan to call your and Taryn's parents right now and tell them so.'

Her own jeans and boots soaked, Taryn made a loud objection. 'You can't do that!'

'I can,' Sandy insisted. 'I also plan to ask your folks to drive out to the ranch tomorrow morning and take you both away from here.'

'But we have three more days!' Jimmy's voice cracked and he yelped like a puppy.

'Not any more, you don't. I want you to go to your cabins and pack your things.' No arguments, no pleading was permitted. Sandy turned on her heel and strode away.

'My dad's gonna kill me!' Taryn wailed.

Jimmy too looked genuinely scared. 'Yeah, and it's down to you!' He spun round and picked on Lacey one last time. 'All because you can't hack it with the rest of us, you have to go and make trouble!'

'Cut it out, Jimmy!' Cory muttered. She took Lacey's boot from Taryn and offered it to its owner. 'Just don't listen!' she advised.

'Yeah, Lacey Darwin was trouble from day one!' Taryn sneered.

Jamming her foot into her boot, Lacey shook her head miserably. 'What did I do?'

'Don't even think about it!' Kirstie backed Cory. 'Those two are going home. They're history!'

'Yeah, and we're staying to have a good time!' Cory outstared Jimmy and challenged him to back off.

'Oh really?' Taryn cut in-between them, shoving Cory out of the way. She eyeballed a trembling Lacey. 'You tell me what kind of good time you're gonna have without your wonderful horse, Lacey Darwin!'

Panic shot into Lacey's eyes. 'I don't know what you're talking about!'

'Gunsmoke! Didn't Meredith Kohler let you in on it? They're taking him back to Bonney Lake!'

'No!' Kirstie jumped in, tried to grab Lacey's arm. But Lacey put out a hand to push her away.

'I don't believe you!' she gasped.

Taryn threw back her head and laughed scornfully. 'Ask anyone! Aah, didn't you know? The Kohlers changed their minds about selling him.

'So you can kiss goodbye to your precious Paso Fino. *Adios*, Gunsmoke. Poor little Lacey has no horse to ride!'

5

In a rockfall on the mountains, Kirstie had witnessed how one loose stone could knock into the next and dislodge a bigger stone, then a still bigger one, until the whole cliff face just seemed to disintegrate and tumble down.

This Lacey Darwin thing was like that, she thought as she watched Jimmy and Taryn's parents stand in the yard talking with Sandy Scott.

The adults, who had flown then driven through most of the night to make it to Half-Moon ranch by nine a.m., looked stern and disappointed, while the two kids hung with difficulty on to a brash, couldn't-care-less act.

Kirstie's mom went through events one last time, with the parents nodding, and Taryn and Jimmy looking sullenly at their feet.

'We're dealing with a difficult situation here,' Sandy explained. 'All types of young riders come to us for Kids' Week from all over America. They have to learn to get along.'

Taryn's father assured her he understood. 'I hear what you say. And no way will I permit Taryn to come on another vacation until I'm satisfied she can act like a decent human being!'

Ouch! Kirstie felt that. The weird thing was, looking at Taryn's folks – her grey-haired, military style father and her small, mouse-like mother – she almost began to feel sorry for her. But not enough to step forward and say goodbye when Robo-Dad ushered his daughter into the car.

Taryn stared out of the window, blank-faced, not even glancing round at Jimmy as the Mercedes drove away.

'What happens now?' Mrs Masterson asked Sandy. She seemed to want to put right some of the things that her son had done. Her Deep South accent was courteous; there wasn't a hair out of place on her streaked blonde head or a single crease in her tailored pants.

'You mean with Lacey?' Sandy's frown deepened and she shook her head. 'Who knows?'

'But you'll call me if there's any news?' Jimmy's mother opened the passenger door for him without looking in his direction. 'I need to know that she's gonna be OK.'

If she is, it's no thanks to your boy! Kirstie thought grimly. Personally she was glad she would never have to see Jimmy Masterson ever again.

As the second car drove off and Sandy too heaved a sigh of relief, Kirstie thought back over the events since yesterday's cook-out.

There was Taryn delivering the false news about Gunsmoke, then no time to stop Lacey and explain the truth before the distressed girl had run off to her cabin.

Sandy had carried out her word to call Taryn's and Jimmy's parents. Cory and Kirstie had gone after Lacey.

Kirstie pressed action replay.

'Open the door, Lacey!' They'd arrived breathless at the door of Trail's End, knocked loudly, received no reply.

'Maybe she's not here after all?' Cory had suggested.

They'd listened for two, maybe three minutes without hearing a sound. Then they'd retreated and reported back to Sandy.

'Leave it. Give Lacey some space,' Kirstie's mom had decided.

'But, Mom, I'm worried she's gonna do something stupid!' Kirstie had Lacey's expression engraved inside her head: a look of horror when she learned that Gunsmoke was to go back to Bonney Lake, turning to betrayal when she glanced in Kirstie's direction.

'What *kind* of stupid?' Sandy had queried.

'I don't know. Just something!'

But her mom had reckoned that Lacey would make it through the crisis and everything would work out. They'd even gone back to the chores, clearing up after the cook-out, checking the horses in the meadow then cleaning out the corral ready for the next day's rides.

'Hey, it's not your problem,' Brad had told Kirstie when he'd finished with Little Vixen and stalled her in the barn for the night. He'd noticed Kirstie raking the yard, still brooding over Lacey's latest disappearance. 'And listen, the kid will be OK when she hears that the blue roan stays after all. Tomorrow morning she gets another lesson from me; we already fixed it up. You see, she'll do just fine!'

Kirstie had said she hoped he was right, then wandered out to the meadow one last time. Which was when she'd discovered what had been in Lacey's head ever since Taryn had dumped her last load of insults on her.

Action replay again. Press the pause button.

Kirstie was at the gate looking for Lucky. The sun was setting behind dark clouds on the horizon, turning the edges of the black masses bright gold, shooting rays of pink light into the pale blue sky.

A movement at the far side of the meadow attracted her attention. Her palomino's pale mane and tail stood out in the dusk as he crossed the pasture swiftly in what looked like an agitated state. Some other horses – Squeaky and Jitterbug, Crazy Horse and Cadillac – circled restlessly by the fence.

'What happened? Where's Gunsmoke?' Kirstie said out loud.

Lucky came to a halt, tossed his head, turned and trotted away.

Gunsmoke should be with Lucky. The two of them had decided to be friends. Lucky was the type of horse to take another under his wing and take care of him until the rest of the ramuda accepted him. So where was Gunsmoke now?

She searched Red Fox Meadow for the blue roan, trying to pick out his dappled coat amongst the sorrels and bays, the greys and spotted Appaloosas.

'He's not here!' she gasped.

Action replay. Slow motion.

Kirstie's first thought was that the Kohlers had reacted badly to Sandy's news that there was no deal to be made. They must have driven right over from Mineville and snuck in with a trailer to whisk the horse away. Low-down, lousy thieves!

But no. Even Meredith Kohler and her smiling mom wouldn't stoop that low.

So the second thought struck Kirstie.

'Lacey saddled him up and took him for a ride!'

Pause button. Then fast forward.

Kirstie sprinted to the tack-room. Gunsmoke's saddle and bridle were gone.

Yeah, Lacey had broken the first rule of the ranch. She'd ridden off alone.

'At night!' When Kirstie broke the news to Ben, the head wrangler had shaken his head in disbelief. 'The kid's crazy!'

But Kirstie had convinced him. They'd checked the meadow a second time, found a clear set of hoofprints leading along Five Mile Creek Trail.

And this was when the rockfall picture first came into Kirstie's mind; one event setting off another, rolling faster and faster, out of control.

'Don't worry, we'll find her!' Brad had promised.

He, Sandy and Charlie had come running when Ben and Kirstie had raised the alarm.

'It's gonna be dark!' Kirstie couldn't believe the craziness.

And it was her fault. She should've made Lacey stop and listen, explained to her that Taryn was lying about Gunsmoke, that things had changed and that Sandy had decided to keep the blue roan at Half-Moon Ranch.

If only! she'd thought.

And she still blamed herself now, after a whole night had passed and there was still no news of the missing girl.

Matt had stayed home from college while Lachelle drove his car into Denver. His plan was to lend support to Sandy and Brad, while Ben, Hadley and Charlie had taken charge of the trail-rides. The remaining kids had set out in subdued mood, promising to keep a sharp lookout for the runaway. But Kirstie knew the scale of those mountains and the difficulty of tracking a single set of hoofprints across stretches of bare granite or through thick stands of ponderosa pines where daylight never penetrated. She'd waved off Cory Shaw's Advanced group with a tight feeling of anxiety and dwindling hope.

'I took another call from Lacey's mom,' Matt reported to Sandy, Ben and Kirstie as they stood discussing tactics outside the barn.

The ranch had made contact with the family some twelve hours earlier, as night had drawn in and the chances of finding Lacey and Gunsmoke straight away had faded. At the same time, they'd alerted the Forest Rangers and a rescue team based in San Luis, who were already out scouring the National Forest tracks and circling overhead in two helicopters flown in from Denver.

On top of all this activity, Sheriff Larry Francini, upholder of law and order in San Luis County, was right then on his way out to the ranch.

'What did Mrs Darwin say?' Kirstie's mom muttered, gazing up the narrow valley as if in hope that Lacey and the blue roan would magically materialise in the morning mist.

Matt strode in to the tack-room to fetch a saddle for Cadillac. 'She and Lacey's stepdad plan to be here by midday.'

'How come it's taking them so long?' Kirstie wanted to know. The family lived south-east of Denver, only three or four hours' drive from Half-Moon Ranch.

'Some problem with their business. They should get free pretty soon and make the drive fast as they can.'

'Huh.' Kirstie turned and waited for instructions from Sandy.

'We ride out in pairs,' her mom decided. 'Me and Matt, and you and Brad.'

'Wouldn't it be better to split up and ride out in four different directions?'

'No. We need to be in pairs in case we come across Lacey and we find she's in trouble. One person stays with her while the other organises help. Get it?'

Kirstie nodded.

'You got a radio?' Sandy checked with Brad.

'Yep.' He tapped his jacket pocket. 'How about we take Miners' Ridge and the territory up by Monument Rock?'

'Sure. We know Lacey headed out by the creek, but we lose the trail by Hummingbird Rock.' This much had been established before nightfall, Wednesday. 'Smiley and another Ranger have taken the jeep road over to Horseshoe Creek and Jim Mullins' place. Matt and I will try Elk Rock and Elk Pass to the north-east.'

'Do you have to wait for Sheriff Francini?' Kirstie had already mounted Lucky.

'Yeah. Now, remember the bottom line. Don't put yourself or your horse in danger for any reason whatsoever; OK?' Sandy knew her daughter's tendency to throw caution to the wind. 'No way do I want to call out the rescue teams for you and Lucky!'

Kirstie managed a small grin as she promised to take care.

With their plans laid, she and Brad set off out of the corral, over the footbridge and along the side of the meadow. Once their horses were eased out of their overnight stiffness and their muscles were warmed, the two riders went at a steady lope along the flat land, Lucky leading and Little Vixen tucked in close behind.

At the fork in the trail leading north-west to

Hummingbird Rock they turned away from the creek, scattering a small herd of mule deer; five or six splendidly antlered bucks who were making the most of the easy grazing before the snows came. The grey-brown creatures scattered through the aspens, black tail tips bobbing above their white rumps.

'Does Lacey know this trail?' Brad asked, still loping smoothly and coming up alongside Kirstie.

'Sure. She rode out to the Canyon with Ben's Advanced group on Tuesday.' As they gained height, Kirstie noticed Charlie's group of beginners wending their way along a trail to their right. The dude visitors rode nose to tail along a safe, wide track on the steadiest of the ranch's quarter-horses.

'Y'know, we can pick up the Paso Fino's route pretty easy,' the reining expert reminded her. 'Gunsmoke has that crazy gait which is simple to follow once we pick up the trail.'

'*If* we pick up the trail!' Kirstie ducked under an overhanging branch and loped on as far as the domed, granite bulk of Hummingbird Rock. With all this rescue activity going on in the sky overhead, and with the roar of the Rangers' jeeps to alert Lacey, Kirstie was guessing that the girl would be making pretty sure to disguise her whereabouts.

She tried to imagine the runaway's state of mind; the way she'd lost it completely over the final run-in with Taryn and Jimmy and made this crazy, suicidal run for it with Gunsmoke. Fourteen hours later, with heavy clouds rolling in over the Peak and the temperature staying low in a bleak westerly wind, Kirstie guessed that Lacey was feeling cold and scared.

But she wasn't the type of kid to turn around and admit defeat. In her head she would be thinking that Gunsmoke's life depended on her riding him to safety, keeping him away from Bonney Lake and his neglectful, greedy owners.

'Are we sure that Jimmy and Taryn don't play any more part in this?' Brad too was wondering exactly what had happened in the gap between the thing with Lacey's boots and her decision to ride off on Gunsmoke. 'Like, did they get at her again when no one was looking; tip her right over the edge?'

Kirstie shook her head as they skirted Dead Man's Canyon and rose out of the pine trees along Miners' Ridge. 'No. Mom asked them to go straight to their cabins, which they did. Lacey must've waited until the yard was clear, taken Gunsmoke's saddle and bridle from the empty tack-room and snuck off without anyone noticing. I did wonder about Meredith Kohler and her mom, though.'

'You think they showed up again?'

'Maybe.' They could have driven over and maybe intercepted the runaways by chance, then confronted Lacey, but she doubted it. 'We'd be talking kidnapping *and* horse stealing then.'

'So?' Brad's frown made clear what he thought of the Kohlers. 'Say they met up by accident. When the poor kid refused to listen, what would they do? They'd grab the horse and put him in the trailer. Then, because they don't give a damn about anything except the Paso Fino, they'd drive off and leave Lacey to find her own way back to the ranch.'

'Only, Lacey can't make it before dark. She has an accident and there she is, stuck down the bottom of a ravine with a broken leg – or worse!' Kirstie drew in a sharp breath and halted Lucky at the end of the ridge. 'Brad, maybe we'd better radio Mom to tell Larry Francini to check out the Kohlers before he does anything else!'

'Good thinking.' He pulled the radio from his

pocket and passed on the message. 'I don't like this sky,' he commented as they prepared to ride on along Bear Hunt Overlook. He was gazing up at Eagle's Peak and what looked like storm clouds gathering over its conical summit. The huge, heavy clouds were the colour of purple bruises, the mountain a bare and brooding presence.

The clatter of a chopper blade grew louder as a heavy-bellied machine rose over a ridge to the far side of the San Luis River. The 'copter tilted and circled above the trees, making both Little Vixen and Lucky dance edgily off the narrow trail. Kirstie reined Lucky back on course. 'A storm is just what we don't need!' she muttered.

Thunder. Lightning. Torrents of water forming on the upper slopes, running like small rivers down the rocks. The flash floods would carry pebbles along in a rapid current, scraping away all remaining signs of Lacey and Gunsmoke's presence.

If they were still up here. If they had got this far. If you ignored the Kohlers and their low-down motives. If, if, if . . .

As Kirstie moved her palomino forward into the shadow of Monument Rock, the first heavy, cold drops of the threatened storm began to fall.

6

There was wet, as in a summer shower when light rain sprinkled your hair and shoulders, and a rainbow promised its pot of gold if you rode over one more ridge or climbed the last few feet out of the low mist and cloud.

And there was wet, as in now. Soaking, shuddering, teeth-clenching wet, when the rain battered the brim of your stetson and mocked any means of protection man might have cared to dream up. It penetrated the seams of slickers, streamed down your face and neck, drenched your pants and filled your boots. The drops hurtled down not separately but in grey sheets, driven at a forty-five degree angle against your body, making you hunch forward and pity your horse, who took the full force of the storm.

'Easy, Lucky!' Kirstie whispered as she reined him under the shelter of an overhanging rock.

The palomino hung his head, his mane darkened and dripping, droplets falling from his eyelids, runnels sliding down his beautiful golden neck and across his strong withers.

'How is he with thunder and lightning?' Brad asked, his handsome face almost unrecognisable as he screwed up his features, then ran the back of his leather-gloved hand across his eyes and forehead.

'Not good,' Kirstie admitted. No horse liked to be out in a storm. His instinct was to turn and run for home. And Lucky was no different, fearing the sudden, forked flashes that stabbed the earth, the echoing roll of noise that shook the heavens.

'Little Vixen likewise.' Brad and his champion black-and-white paint crept under the shelter with Kirstie.

As yet, the worst of the storm had clung to the mountain and only sent its squalls of torrential rain sweeping down the valleys towards Monument Rock. But both Brad and Kirstie were clear that it was only a matter of time before the real McCoy set in.

Huddled against the rock, Lucky threw back his head, opened his mouth wide and let out a high whinny.

Down below, a horse from one of the trail-riding groups replied. Soon a series of equine calls and answers rang out down the hillside.

'Just checking!' Kirstie quipped. 'They need to tell the other guys they're not alone.'

'Yeah, I wonder if one of those squealers could be old Gunsmoke,' Brad murmured. He held Vixen on a short rein in case she took it into her head to bolt. The paint grew more and more uneasy under the black ledge as the first faint rolls of thunder rattled down from Eagle's Peak.

'I hope!' Kirstie muttered. 'Maybe this storm will drive him and Lacey back to the ranch.'

'Say that like you mean it.'

'OK. I'm not convinced,' she confessed. She could feel the cold rain trickling down her spine and her heart beginning to thump uneasily as the storm took hold.

'See how the horses pick up our fear.' Brad

noticed Lucky's ears flatten and his eyes begin to roll. Little Vixen meanwhile struggled for her head and pranced sideways, sending a shower of small stones bouncing down the slope.

And the rain kept on coming; driving sheet after sheet. Within minutes it had filled the tumbling creeks to overflowing, spilling over rocks to create a treacherous, slippery moss surface. And it hammered against the scaly trunks of the trees, sent bleating pikas scuttling from sodden rock to rock, their brown fur drenched and sticking to their skinny ribs.

Then it came – a brilliant fork of lightning splitting the black sky. *Crash!* Thunder followed close on its heels; at first a narrow, eardrum-shattering crack, broadening to a roar, tailing off in a long, low rumble.

Lucky whirled then reared on to his hind legs, tipping Kirstie back in the saddle. A panicking Vixen squealed and tried to wrench the reins from Brad's experienced hands.

'That storm is gonna pass right over our heads!' Brad gasped. As he spoke, a thick crackle from the two-way radio in his pocket told them that someone from the ranch was trying to get in contact.

He took out the radio, flicked a switch and spoke. 'Brad here. Over.'

'Brad, this is Sandy. I want you and Kirstie to come down. Over.'

No way! Kirstie shook her head and mouthed the words. She wanted to carry on the search.

'Can't we stay here under Bear Hunt Overlook and wait for the storm to pass? Over.'

'No can do, Brad. I already brought the trail-riders in. I want you and the horses off the mountain pronto. Over.'

'That only leaves the Forest Rangers and the choppers continuing the rescue operation. We're not happy with that. Over.'

'Tough, I'm afraid. I already told Kirstie not to get involved in anything dangerous, remember? And the weather forecast is for a bad storm; high winds and flash floods. Like I said, I want everyone off there. Over.'

Brad shrugged at Kirstie. 'I hear you. We'll be right down. Over.'

As he pocketed the radio, another flash of lightning tore through the sky and thunder ripped down the valley. The horses jumped and lashed out with their back legs.

'Whoa, easy!' Brad tried to soothe Vixen,

whose tail whipped from side to side and who regained her balance only to freak out again as yet another flash illuminated the sky. 'C'mon!' he told Kirstie. 'We're outta here!'

So they retraced their steps in the driving rain which buffeted them from behind. It ballooned out their slickers, making them flap and adding to the horses' distress.

'Once we make it down Miners' Ridge into the canyon, the wind should be less!' Kirstie yelled at Brad as once more she let her horse lead the way.

A crash of thunder drove Vixen sideways against a tree, trapping her rider's lower leg between her flank and the trunk. Brad grimaced and pushed them both clear.

And Kirstie's optimism turned out to be misplaced as they came down off the ridge into the deep ravine of Dead Man's Canyon. She knew from the past, when a bunch of wild horses had sought shelter from a storm right here, that the bottom of the culvert soon filled with rainwater which then streamed with great force towards a rocky outlet where it joined forces with a hidden waterfall.

So, though the wind did die down, the danger was that they might get caught in a landslide as the rain loosened the soil at the sides of the ravine. Earth, stones, small branches and uprooted bushes would come swirling down; another shock for the horses as the whole landscape seemed to shift and become treacherous underfoot.

'Gee!' Brad fought with Vixen to get her across a muddy ditch.

Kirstie had already walked Lucky through the foaming brown stream. It had been knee-deep, the far bank clogged with mud and sodden fallen leaves. She felt the hairs at the back of her neck prickle as, behind her, the terrified paint stumbled into the water, fell on to her knees, then picked herself up and staggered on.

'OK?' she checked with Brad. 'She didn't go lame, did she?'

He walked her a little way towards the exit to the canyon. 'I guess not.'

More lightning darted overhead, striking a tree on the ridge which they'd just walked. The stricken pine, less than half a mile from where they were now, cracked from top to bottom. It split with a terrific tearing of wood and a swoosh of collapsing branches, leaving only a raw black stump pointing skywards as the rest of the tree crashed down the sheer drop into Dead Man's Canyon.

'Our next problem is Fat Man's Squeeze!' Kirstie gasped, shaken by the sight of the charred, ruined tree. The force of nature was a pretty scary phenomenon. 'There's bound to be a flash flood through there!'

Sure enough, the tight gulley was awash. Water came up to Lucky's belly with a force strong enough to carry large logs which had jammed across the gap.

'What do we do?' she asked. The logs looked like a beaver had been at work constructing a strong dam.

Quickly Brad dismounted and handed her Little Vixen's reins. He splashed waist-deep through the flood and began to wrench at the log-jam, casting loose debris to one side until it was possible for the horses to step through the Squeeze. 'Lead Vixen, and better make it quick!' he urged. 'I can see another heavy log heading our way!'

Grabbing a stout branch, he hoisted himself on a ledge and wielded it, ready to lever the approaching log off-course.

'C'mon, Vixen!' Kirstie clicked her tongue and

tried to lead the horse on. At the same time, Lucky pulled back from the narrow gap, fearing that the current would be too strong for him to make it through.

'It's OK, I got the log!' Brad called as the two pieces of wood collided and he bounced the log away. Then he leaped down from the ledge and leap-frogged on to Vixen's back, giving her a smart slap on the backside which drove her forward and in turn bundled Lucky ahead of her through the Squeeze.

'We made it; good boy!' Kirstie breathed as they came out the far side. The land opened up on to a gentler slope which would lead them down to Hummingbird Rock where they could join a jeep road and travel more quickly back to the safety and shelter of the ranch.

'Not yet, we didn't!' Brad cringed under a fierce flash of lightning and the loudest crack of thunder so far. The storm, directly overhead, battered them harder than ever before.

This time, both horses were driven crazy. They arched their backs and bucked, heads between their knees, back legs kicking out in terror. Vixen squealed and threw herself around; Lucky bucked again, tossing Kirstie out of the saddle and forcing her to grip the horn with both hands so that she landed off-balance, but still on his back.

Then, when the electric flash had forked its way to earth and the thunder had exhausted itself, the wind and the rain came blasting down from the mountain, almost sweeping the two riders out of the saddle.

'Kirstie, watch out!' A cry from behind coincided with the splitting, tearing sound of an entire tree being destroyed.

She sensed rather than saw a pine tree tilt, its snake-like roots ripped from the thin soil, its trunk toppling against another tree, branches tearing

off and beginning to crash down on top of her and Lucky.

'Move it!' she cried, digging her hooves into the paralysed palomino's sides.

Showered by autumn leaves and torn twigs, with one branch falling earthwards, she galvanised him into action, escaping just in time for it to land six feet behind them. It thudded into a bed of pine needles with a rush and rustle of twigs that would linger inside her head for days to come.

'Kirstie, what happened?' Brad's voice called from the far side of the toppled branch.

'We're OK. Thanks!' Her breath came short and sharp. Lucky's whole body quivered, but they were both unharmed.

Rounding the limb of the tree with Vixen, Brad looked relieved to see them in one piece. He trotted alongside, tipping water from the brim of his hat and pointing their little group towards home.

'I can see why Sandy wanted us down from the mountain!' he muttered, glancing warily at the lowering sky. For a few moments, the lightning had stopped and the thunder rolled quietly into the distance. But the rain came down in buckets and whole slopes ran with six inches of excess water.

It was no time to sit and think about lucky escapes. Instead, they gritted their teeth and splashed on.

'Steer clear of the trees from now on!' Kirstie reminded Brad. She felt tired to death, either from the trauma of the falling branch or from battling with the horses in the storm. Maybe both. She set her sights on Hummingbird Rock. Beyond that, there was a thirty minute ride until they reached the ranch.

'Yeah,' he agreed, equally numb and exhausted.

Kirstie eased into a steady trot, looking out in every direction for more branches about to fall on her head. Thirty minutes away from heat and dry clothes. With Lacey Darwin and Gunsmoke still lost. She sighed and set her face for home. 'Because if the wind don't get us, the lightning sure will!'

Sheriff Larry Francini looked the same as always, like nothing ever disturbed him or made him break out into a sweat. He sat in the Scotts' kitchen listening to the exact circumstances of Lacey's disappearance.

When? Why? These were his main questions.

'I can answer the first, but only guess at the second,' Sandy had to admit. The thunderstorm clung stubbornly to the area around Half-Moon Ranch, caught on the peaks and still rolling down the valleys. Everywhere was standing in water – the deserted corral and yard, the meadow where the horses huddled together for comfort.

Everyone except Lacey Darwin was safely home, including Brad and Kirstie, who had been the last to arrive. There was hot chocolate, dry clothes waiting, someone to whisk the horses into the barn and take care of them while the two riders dried out.

'So guess away,' Larry told Sandy. 'Why would a kid risk her neck by riding off at night?'

With Smiley Gilpin, the Forest Ranger, and Luther Irving, the leader of the helicopter rescue squad, listening in around the kitchen table, Kirstie's mom explained Lacey's problem home-life and her thoughtless treatment at the hands of Jimmy and Taryn.

'The two issues combined together made her try something stupid,' Sandy told them. 'Plus the fact that Lacey was under the impression that

Gunsmoke, her favourite horse, was on his way back to the Kohlers.'

'Yeah, I got news from Bonney Lake,' the sheriff confided. 'I sent along Tim Foster, my deputy, to speak with Estelle Kohler and her daughter, Meredith. Tim let me know that they have the perfect alibi for the time last night when this all went off.'

'What is it?' Kirstie asked. She sat by the stove in sweater and fresh jeans, clasping her mug of chocolate.

'They were home watching a video – *The Horse Whisperer*. Kinda ironic, huh? Mr Kohler and at least two of his hired helpers working on some new fencing around the place can validate that.'

'Hmm.' She glanced at Brad, who stood quietly by the door with Matt and Ben. So much for that theory.

'Besides, Tim described Meredith's reaction to the news that her precious Gunsmoke had gone missing.' Sheriff Francini smoothed his dark moustache, then stroked his bald head. 'According to him, the girl was in shock. There were tears and wild talk of suing Half-Moon Ranch for failing to take proper care of the horse.'

'For God's sake!' Sandy stood up quickly with a loud scrape of her chair.

'Don't pay no attention,' Larry recommended. 'All I'm saying is, it would seem to put the Kohlers out of the picture.'

There was a heavy silence until Luther Irving and Smiley began a muttered discussion of how long it would be before the thunderstorm played itself out. Luther decided he couldn't send up the choppers again until the weather improved, while Smiley said he would give it another fifteen minutes before he drove out afresh with the Jeep.

Meanwhile, Kirstie found she couldn't sit and do nothing. She got up and wandered out on to the porch, standing looking at the rain and a solitary figure draped in waterproofs making its way down from the cabins towards the ranch house. Only when Cory Shaw stepped right up on to the porch beside her did she finally recognise who it was.

The Texan girl threw back her oilskin hood and shook out her fair hair. 'No news?'

'Nothing,' Kirstie sighed. 'We're expecting the Darwins to show up as soon as they can make it down the dirt road in this weather. Then things really get hard.'

'Yeah. They're gonna go ape when they see this territory,' Cory added. She braced herself at a bright flash of lightning and a fresh crack of thunder. 'I heard Mr Darwin is a pretty scary guy.'

'Who told you that; Lacey?'

Cory nodded. 'They don't get on. He runs a twenty-four hour gas station out on the Interstate south of Denver and he makes Lacey's mom work there some nights. It means Lacey gets left home alone.'

'Not good,' Kirstie murmured. Rain bounced off the barn roof and ran noisily down the gutters.

'Lacey told me she'd rather die than go back home after this vacation.'

'She did?' Kirstie turned sharply.

'Yeah. I guess I didn't take her seriously at the time. Now I'm not so sure.' Cory's voice was sad, her expression loaded with guilt.

'Well, I sure look forward to meeting Mr Darwin!' Kirstie said grimly, looking out for a car coming through the entrance up the hill.

But there was another half hour to wait before it finally happened, during which time the storm began to ease and the rescue teams started to reorganise. Kirstie was insisting to Sandy that she and Lucky were both fit to ride out again and join the afternoon search when a muddy black Chrysler slid down the slope and into the yard.

Everyone stopped and froze awkwardly, leaving Sandy to walk forward to greet the couple who stepped out of the car. Only Kirstie followed uncertainly in her wake.

'Mrs Darwin? I'm Sandy Scott.' Offering to shake hands, Kirstie's mom spoke urgently but quietly.

'I'm Carol Darwin. This is my husband, Steve.' The woman glanced calmly round. 'We couldn't get overnight help for the gas station, so we were held up. Otherwise we would've driven here earlier. Then we were caught in the storm in San Luis. So what's new?'

'Nothing, I have to tell you.' Sandy confided the disappointing information.

Kirstie watched Carol Darwin's smooth forehead crease. Behind the neatly styled auburn hair and the well turned out appearance of Mrs Darwin's dark blue jacket and narrow trousers, she thought she detected a careworn air.

'Listen!' Steve Darwin spoke for the first time. He came over as a man with no free time, always taking life at a run. He was tall, dark, a little overweight, about forty-five years old. 'You know Lacey has pulled this disappearing stunt before?'

'She did?' The information interested Larry Francini very much. He stepped out from the porch in his white stetson, wearing the silver star on his zip-up jacket. 'How many times did Lacey run away from home?'

'Twice.' Mr Darwin pulled an apologetic face, looking round at the rescue teams which had congregated in the yard. 'She came back voluntarily both times.'

'She did, huh?' The sheriff took this in without any obvious reaction. Would this surprising fact make him decide to scale down the search, Kirstie wondered.

'Come inside for coffee,' Sandy offered, leading the way and sounding hopeful. 'If you can tell us more about Lacey's pattern of behaviour, maybe we have a better chance of finding her this time also.'

Brad and Matt came up alongside Kirstie as the sheriff, Sandy and the Darwins disappeared into the house. 'Are they saying she makes a habit of this kind of thing?' Matt checked, shaking his head as he slowly followed the others inside. 'No wonder the parents didn't exactly bust a gut racing to get out here!'

'Yeah, but . . . !' Kirstie didn't follow the logic behind this sudden lessening of anxiety. She turned to Brad. 'Surely the fact that Lacey did this twice before makes it worse, not better!'

'You would think,' he agreed. 'Except she showed up of her own accord those two times, remember.'

'Yeah.' Kirstie's response came more slowly. She was almost talking to herself as she let her gaze wander over the yard to the helicopters stationed beyond the barn, the Jeeps and the rescuers hanging around in the tack-room porch waiting for the torrential rain to clear.

'She came back before, but maybe not this time.'

The situation wasn't the same. Those two previous times, Taryn and Jimmy hadn't figured. And neither had Gunsmoke. Before, it had only been down to the fact that Carol Darwin had remarried and her new husband kept her out working nights. Bad enough, but not the absolute end.

'One: this time Lacey ran away up a mountain at night,' she reminded herself under her breath.

'Two: she headed into one of the worst storms of the year. Three: she told Cory she would rather die than go back home.'

No; those parents were wrong to try and convince the sheriff that this was just another half-hearted, attention-seeking trick. Kirstie gave herself a firm talking-to. 'Because last and not least, she rode out on Gunsmoke. That alone is enough for me!'

7

'Consider the horse,' Ben said. 'However this turns out, Gunsmoke has been through one heck of a lot – out all night, exposed to the storm. We'll be lucky to get him back in good shape.'

'Fortunately, there's still some grazing left on the meadows,' Sandy pointed out. Then she added wryly, 'And plenty of water in the creeks. So leastways he won't starve.'

As the rain continued to ease, the ever-increasing bunch of people involved in the search for the lost girl and horse congregated in the shelter of the Scotts' new barn. Minutes were ticking by; it was two-thirty in the afternoon and time, Kirstie realised, to switch their attention from Lacey's reasons for disappearing and focus in on the behaviour of one scared and confused Paso Fino. She seized on the head wrangler's change of emphasis and ran with it inside her own head.

Consider the horse. Well, for starters, horses had better night vision than humans by far. Genetics equipped them to spot predators such as mountain lions and coyotes lurking in the shadows of rocks or under trees. And they could hear real well too. So it might not be too much to hope that Gunsmoke had been able to take care of himself and Lacey all through the previous night on the mountains.

'Lucky we didn't get snow,' she murmured. Though there again, snowfall might have brought the horse back down in search of shelter. 'But it's a pity Gunsmoke don't know the territory too well. He won't have been able to show Lacey where they should hole up when the storm started this morning.'

'Say, can we stop talking about the darned horse and concentrate on the kid?' Steve Darwin was pacing up and down the central aisle of the barn, impatiently waiting for the decision to restart the search.

'The two go together,' Matt pointed out, turning from a discussion with Brad and Ben about the possibility that Lacey and Gunsmoke had made it to an old cattle station round the far side of Eagle's Peak.

'How about the old mine workings along Bear Hunt Overlook?' Hadley chipped in. 'A horse could find shelter in the entrance to one of those tunnels.'

Kirstie shook her head. 'Brad and me rode up there this morning. There was no sign of anybody breaking down a door to get inside.'

'Any deserted cabins along Timberline Trail this time of year?' Sheriff Francini asked Smiley Gilpin. The squat litle lawman seemed to be permanently observing the Darwins out of the corner of his eye.

'A couple. But we already drove along there and we didn't find nothing.' The ranger's ruddy, outdoors face was concerned, marked by a tight frown between his fair eyebrows.

'How come we're going round in circles?' Steve Darwin asked, frustration oozing out of every pore. 'A kid can't just vanish up a mountain. The sooner we get out there again and locate them, the sooner we can all pack up and go home!'

'Steve!' Carol Darwin tugged the sleeve of his brown leather jacket. 'These people are doing all they can!'

'No, Steve is right,' Luther Irving agreed. He'd come back from taking a look at the sky and using the helicopter radio to tune into the latest local weather forecast. 'Things are looking good for the rest of the day. So come on, guys, let's see some action!'

There was a sudden breaking up of the groups inside the barn. Smiley and two other rangers took off for their Jeeps; Ben began to organise tack for fresh horses to continue the search.

'I could take Johnny Mohawk; give Lucky some time out,' Kirstie suggested to her mom, determined not to miss out.

Sandy was considering the options when one of the men from the chopper rescue team sidled up to them at the exit to the barn.

'Hey, Mrs Scott. I'm Dan Borne.' He was a square-shouldered, rugged-looking guy wearing a baseball cap and a beaten-up lumberjack jacket.

From the way he frowned and glanced nervously around, Kirstie guessed he had something he wanted to say in private. 'I'll go get Johnny!' she told her mom.

Sandy grabbed her by the arm. 'No, Kirstie, hold it. Hey, Dan, how're you doing?'

'Not great, Mrs Scott. I've been out with Luther and the other guys, but I got something on my mind.'

'So spit it out.' Aware that the two chopper engines were starting up and that the volunteer rescuer had limited time to come across with the goods, Sandy pressed him to speak out.

'It won't sound good, what I have to tell you,' Dan confessed. His wide face flushed red; his grey eyes rested anywhere but Sandy's inquisitive face. 'This is gonna land me in a heap of trouble, I know. Listen, I work part of the time for Walter Kohler out at Bonney Lake.'

The words worked like an electric jolt running through Kirstie's nervous system. *Not the Kohlers again!* The name kept on cropping up.

'I've been building fences for him, along with Ed Jessop. Mr Kohler hires us by the hour. He used Ed and me as an alibi when Tim Foster showed up at his place this morning.'

Sandy nodded. 'The sheriff said you backed up the Kohlers' story that they were at home during the time Lacey and Gunsmoke vanished.'

'Ed did,' Dan confirmed. 'I left early to come help with the rescue, so I wasn't there. But Tim radioed the chopper for back-up from me, and I ... well, I guess I just took the easy way out!'

'You said the Kohlers were watching a video?' Kirstie stared at Dan Borne. 'Now you're saying that's not true?'

Sheepishly he nodded. 'I feel bad, like I said. But Walter Kohler pays my wages. He don't pay well and he don't always pay on time, but I got rent to find, a family to support. When he put me on the spot back there, I just went along with the story he was giving the deputy sheriff.'

'So what really happened late yesterday?' Sandy cut in. 'Were any of the Kohlers home like they claimed?'

'No, ma'am, they were not,' Dan answered quietly, small nerves clicking and jumping along his tense jawline. 'About four-thirty to five, maybe fifteen minutes before me and Ed packed up our stuff and went home for the night, they all three climbed in the trailer and drove off!'

'Yes, yes, you take Johnny Mohawk!' Sandy had gasped at Kirstie before she ran off to give Larry

Francini the latest news. 'Get Ben to saddle up Jitterbug for Brad. The two of you can ride out together again!'

'I knew it!' Kirstie cried as soon as she and Brad were out on the trail. The clouds were lifting and lightening, still clinging to the ravines but allowing a pale sunlight to struggle through. 'I *knew* Meredith Kohler didn't really fall apart over Gunsmoke's disappearance. That was all a big act!'

'Little Miss Drama Queen,' Brad muttered. He settled into the saddle, getting used to the sorrel mare's snatched trot then easing her into a lope which was much smoother and faster. 'So what's the big plan now?'

Kirstie caught up with Jitterbug and loped her lively black stallion alongside. Both horses were fresh and eager, covering the ground like crazy. 'I don't know nothing about the big picture; I'm leaving that to Mom and Sheriff Francini. But you and me are heading back to Hummingbird Rock.'

'We are?' Brad made out that Kirstie was the boss, letting her ease Johnny Mohawk ahead as they steered around a pool of water left standing after the morning's storm.

The stallion's heels clipped the edge of the giant puddle and splashed Jitterbug right in the face. The sorrel tossed her head and veered sideways along a small ledge.

'Yee-hah!' Brad was having a good time in spite of the circumstances. He jumped Jitterbug back down on to the trail and loped on after Kirstie and Johnny. 'So, tell a dumb old cowboy how come we're going over ground we already searched?'

'Look at it this way.' Kirstie rode with her horse's loping stride, flexing her knees, feeling a fresh wind in her hair. Ahead of them, the soaked ground steamed in the first sun's rays since the storm. 'The Kohlers get a phone call telling them Lacey has ridden off on Gunsmoke. They already know Mom ain't willing to sell the horse back to them and they're feeling pretty sore. So what do they do? They climb in the trailer, like Dan Borne said; they drive over from Bonney Lake second-guessing which way the runaways might be headed.'

'You think they hit lucky?' Brad asked. Hummingbird Rock was already in sight, rising out of the band of dark pine trees, glinting pink in the sun.

Kirstie nodded. 'Think about it. There aren't too many places you can get a horse-trailer through the forest along the dirt tracks. There's Timberline Trail, which the loggers and Forest Rangers use. There's another track over to Jim Mullin's place in the next valley. And there's the Jeep road by Hummingbird Rock.'

Brad followed her train of thought. 'So why Hummingbird?'

'Because to get along Timberline Trail the Kohlers would have to drive right by Red Eagle Lodge; Smiley's cabin. Someone would've seen the trailer; there would be tyre marks in the mud.'

'Likewise if they took the track to Jim Mullins' ranch?' Brad took the point. 'The only way out would be past the Lazy B, and Jim's guys would've been sure to spot them.'

'Yeah!' The more she thought about it, the more excited Kirstie became. She was sure now that they were close to picking up Gunsmoke and Lacey's trail. 'And Lacey rode the horse along the side of the creek, turning up to the Rock, remember? We lost the prints across that stretch right below us, so we went on towards Miners' Ridge. But that was a bad decision on our part!'

'So now we take a good look at the Jeep road,'

Brad agreed, happy with Kirstie's clear-thinking decision. 'But if we find anything, we radio Sandy and get the others out here, OK?'

The track used by the off-road vehicles skirted around the back of Hummingbird Rock.

Kirstie and Brad had dismounted and tethered their horses, climbed the Rock and were gazing down along the length of the road in both directions.

'The problem is, the storm,' Kirstie sighed. Her excitement of a few minutes earlier was evaporating like the puddles on the ground.

'Yeah, the rain sure wiped out a whole lot of potential clues,' Brad agreed in a slow drawl.

There was mud everywhere. Jitterbug and Johnny were slithering up to their hocks in the stuff. Brad and Kirstie's boots were caked solid.

And still the rain-swollen creeks tumbled over rocks and ran in shallow rivers across the track, erasing every tyre mark and footprint from the gravel surface.

From the top of Hummingbird, Kirstie raised her gaze from the Jeep road and took in the vast stretch of hills and valleys undulating towards the horizon. There was nothing between them and

Eagle's Peak except forest and the occasional meadow; home to mule deer and summer pasture for the cattle on the Lazy B.

She knew that for another couple of miles the narrow road snaked on through the dense trees, finishing at a logging station which was manned only during the summer months. Right now it would be empty and padlocked, awaiting the snowdrifts which would silt up against its windows and door and reach as high as its sloping roof.

'Maybe we should follow the track as far as it goes,' Brad suggested, trying to imagine the way Lacey's mind might have worked when she arrived at this spot late in the evening.

'I'd feel a whole lot happier if we could spot a clue – anything at all!' Kirstie frowned. She slithered down Hummingbird, arms held wide for balance, feeling overwhelmed by the silence and the space around her.

Back on the track, she poked around with the toe of her boot in the undergrowth to either side, disturbing the tall tobacco plants, whose pale husks showered black seeds to the ground. One recent hoofprint, even one tyre mark would help!

Nothing. A pair of tiny, nut-brown hummingbirds, disturbed by the intruders, flew up from a thorn bush, their long beaks sharp as needles, wings beating fast and invisible until they vanished into a tree.

'OK, we ride on.' Despondent, Kirstie remounted Johnny Mohawk and headed up the dark trail, her mood affected partly by the sudden disappearance of the sun behind a new bank of cloud. Gloom returned to the trees, still dripping from the storm.

'Time to – you know what!' Brad reminded her as he rode ahead.

'Yeah. To cowboy up!' She shook herself into a more positive frame of mind, remembering the favourite Half-Moon Ranch phrase when things weren't looking too great.

Time to square your shoulders and press on like the old cowboys on month-long cattle drives. Your butt might be sore, your legs aching in the stirrups, your whole body frozen solid, but those beefs had to be brought down from the hills and driven eastward through the Rocky Mountains and on for winter grazing to the great plains of Kansas.

So, by the time she and Brad arrived at the lonely loggers' station, Kirstie's chin was up and her mind set on finding the evidence they needed that Lacey and Gunsmoke had passed this way.

The wooden station was set on a flat piece of land backed by a culvert of thirty foot high cliffs. The L-shaped cabin was built of sturdy logs, its windows small and shuttered, a narrow porch running the length of one side. The smooth gravel area in front was flanked by stacks of logs some fifteeen feet in length and eight or ten feet high.

Kirstie noticed that though the recently departed loggers must have left everything neat and tidy for the winter, the wind had already blown leaves under the porch and banked them up against the doorstep. They rustled softly as she approached, twisting in a sudden flurry and flying out of the shelter against her horse's legs.

Johnny Mohawk skittered away from the quiet cabin, spooked by the crazy leaves.

'Easy!' Kirstie murmured, sliding from the saddle and tethering him to the porch rail. She glanced around, judging that there was plenty of room for the Kohlers' trailer to have turned and departed, her eyes peeled for a sign that her guess was correct.

'The surface is firm,' Brad pointed out, already dismounted and crunching across the gravel.

'This stuff drains easy; you'd never guess we ever had the storm.'

'Do you see any tyre marks?' Kirstie asked.

'Some.' He pointed them out and gestured her across. 'But not recent,' he decided.

'How come?' She studied the shallow parallel ruts in the ground.

'Because they're ankle deep in fallen aspen leaves.' Brad pointed out the russet and gold debris. 'If they were new, the Kohlers' tyres would've crushed the leaves to a pulp. These were most likely made by the loggers' trucks when they left a week or so back.'

Reluctantly Kirstie had to admit that he was right. But she gritted her teeth and went on looking. 'What about these?' she called to Brad, pointing with her toe at a different type of tyre mark showing where a large, heavy vehicle had executed a three-point turn across the gravel yard.

He squatted to examine them, then nodded. 'Maybe.'

Hopes rekindled, Kirstie was already scrambling up the nearest pile of logs for a better view. She found she could track the tyres out along the Jeep road until they disappeared into a stretch of muddy swamp which the pelting rain and floods had churned up then smoothed away. More exciting still, she spotted a set of hoofprints at the end of the log pile, hidden from the angle at which they'd first approached the cabin.

'Brad!' Her voice came out high and squeaky.

It brought him racing across. 'Hey, maybe . . . just maybe!'

'Never mind maybe; these are Gunsmoke's prints!' Wishful thinking made Kirstie one hundred per cent sure.

She jumped down from the logs and moved in on the precise area, picking out the horseshoe shapes, the divots of gravelly earth churned up by the Paso Fino's feet.

'Looks like the horse got pretty wild,' Brad said slowly. He took off his hat and ran a hand through his dark hair. 'There are boot prints over there; more than one set.'

A horse; several people. Telltale marks in the gravel.

Kirstie pictured it in a flash. Lacey riding blindly through the dusk, choosing the easiest route to put the greatest distance between herself and the ranch before night fell. She'd come across the logging station and greeted it like a small miracle; a place to shelter and rest. Time to think things through before morning.

Then, when she thought she was safe, the Kohlers had showed up with their trailer, cruising the forest tracks, looking for the runaways. If Sandy Scott wouldn't return Gunsmoke to them by fair means, they were determined to try foul.

And their luck had eventually come good. Maybe Lacey had tethered the horse for the night and was already trying to sleep, hunched up on the cold porch, restless and wakeful.

The trailer lights would've startled her and made the blue roan gelding whinny in dismay. Lacey would have jumped up and run to untie the horse, but the Kohlers were already on to her, scuffling to stop her running away again, dead set on dragging Gunsmoke up the ramp of the waiting trailer . . .

What then? Her grey eyes wide with anxiety, Kirstie turned to Brad. 'D'you think the Kohlers got Gunsmoke away after all?'

He frowned then nodded. 'I'd lay a hundred dollar bet they did.'

'So what happened to Lacey? They were only interested in the horse; no way would they want her along!'

'Maybe they took her and dumped her some

place between here and Bonney Lake.' Brad too tried to piece together the full picture. 'But then she'd have been able to run and raise the alarm, and she didn't do that.'

Kirstie took a deep breath. 'D'you reckon they could've harmed her?'

'Jeez, I guess that's another maybe!' To cover his fears, Brad carried on scouting the area behind the log pile.

A scuffle to get the horse into the trailer ... Lacey resisting Walter Kohler, who would be much bigger than her and by all accounts a mean, scary guy ... the struggle getting out of hand ... an angry guy grabbing a nearby rock, raising it above his head, bringing it crashing down!

'Kirstie!' Brad stooped to pick up an object. He brought it towards her, half-stumbling against the log pile in his haste. 'Do you recognise this?'

It was a denim baseball cap, covered in mud, its peak half torn off.

She took it from Brad, turned it over, looked inside at a dark, wet stain.

'It's Lacey's!' she whispered.

Lacey's favourite hat. Trampled and torn. And the dark patch inside the crown was blood.

8

'Brad to Sandy; over!'

'Sandy here. How's it goin'? Over.'

'We found the kid's cap. Looks like she was in some kind of accident or fight. Over.'

There was a crackle and mush on the airwave as Kirstie's mom hesitated, got her thoughts together, then replied. 'I'll let Larry know the score. Do we think the Kohlers are involved? Over.'

'We sure do. The way Kirstie sees it, and given what Dan Borne told us, the three of them jumped at the chance to drive out here and track

Gunsmoke down. Can you find out from the sheriff if his deputy searched their place, or did he settle for asking a few simple questions and taking their word for it that they'd been nowhere near Half-Moon Ranch? Over.'

'Will do, Brad. I guess Larry will want to drive over to Bonney Lake and double-check.' Sandy was evidently taking this latest emergency in her stride. 'Meanwhile, I'll alert the rescue teams and send them your way. What's your exact location? Over.'

Kirstie listened as Brad described the loggers' cabin at the end of the Jeep road. She held the trampled, bloodstained cap in her trembling hand, doing her best to tell herself that Lacey's injury need not be serious; probably a shallow cut that had bled for a bit, then stopped.

'So what's the plan for you and Kirstie? Over.' Sandy sounded anxious lest the two of them raced headlong into a reckless act. Yet there was no time to waste, so she had to trust them to make good decisions.

Brad glanced at Kirstie. 'Your daughter's boss lady round here. I'm putting her on. Over.'

'Mom, hi. I reckon Brad and me should ride out along the Jeep road towards Route 5. Maybe we can pick up some more clues. Over.'

'Good thinkin'. Listen, Kirstie, between us we're gonna make this come good, OK?'

'Sure.'

'Kirstie?'

'Yeah, I'm here. Over.'

'Say that like you mean it. This is gonna come good! Over.'

'I said sure thing, Mom. Over!'

Mother and daughter signed off, and Kirstie and Brad made straight for their horses, eager to follow up their plan of action.

Quickly they mounted and retraced their steps back past the domed hulk of Hummingbird Rock, restricting their pace to a trot, searching the ground for a particular type of tyre mark which they now suspected belonged to the Kohlers' trailer.

But the problem was the same as before: too much rain. They covered three miles of dirt track without picking up even the smallest clue.

Meanwhile, Kirstie was aware of the two rescue choppers following Sandy's directions and rising clumsily over the nearest ridge. As they circled and then picked up the winding road which the Kohlers must have taken, she had the sensation of being trailed by noisy, giant metal dragonflies whose shadows slid over rocks and trees, blades churning, bodies swaying some hundred feet from the ground.

'Easy, Johnny!' Kirstie murmured to her horse. His ears flicked and rotated anxiously towards the oppressive helicopters. They'd come to a stretch of track which narrowed between two high cliffs, with a sharp bend in the middle. A notoriously hard section of road for the loggers' trucks to deal with, she knew that the morning's storm would have done nothing to ease her and Brad's way through.

'Whoa!' Brad saw the difficulty. He reined back Jitterbug to consider how they should tackle a mudslide which had half blocked the route.

'Maybe we could find a higher track?' Kirstie suggested, holding Johnny on a tight rein. The skittish black stallion – half-Arab, half-plain ordinary quarter-horse – danced and pranced sideways into the more dainty sorrel.

'Those cliffs look too steep and slippery to me. I reckon we dismount and lead 'em through the mud.'

Reluctantly Kirstie agreed, knowing that this section would slow them down badly. She also didn't look forward to coming out the far side with her jeans caked with dirt again. But there was nothing else for it.

Brad took the lead, sludging and sliding with Jitterbug across the sloppy mud. 'Jeez, it's like wading through molasses!' he called over his shoulder before he disappeared around the hairpin bend.

Sighing, Kirstie jumped down from the saddle, took hold of the stallion's reins and followed. 'Yeah, I know, Johnny. This ain't my idea of fun either.'

The horse's nostrils had flared; his head had jerked back in disgust. But they were almost round the bend, the track was opening up, the cliffs to either side receding.

'Hey!' She protested as Johnny Mohawk barged her sideways in his anxiety to be back on firm ground. Thrown off balance by the sudden movement, Kirstie had to step into a ditch containing eighteen inches of cold, muddy water.

She splashed and struggled to scramble out, grabbing hold of a broken branch that had been ripped from a nearby aspen. The tree itself was badly damaged, she noticed as she hauled herself on to the track. A recent impact from a large vehicle had tilted the trunk at an angle away from the road; patches of its silver-grey bark were gouged out, leaving deep, ragged scars.

'Brad, come take a look at this!' In her mind's eye she pictured a vehicle as large as a horse-trailer coming to grief on the bend. Maybe it had been going too fast and had slid on the greasy surface, its wheels spinning and skidding into the ditch. Only the aspen tree would have saved it from sliding completely out of control.

'What happened here?' Brad took in the details, kicking around and finding evidence of deep ruts in the mud. Though they'd been partly washed away by the storm, it was still clear that a truck had indeed landed itself in deep trouble.

'See these scrape marks along the rock?' Kirstie pointed to where chunks of granite were chipped away through contact with metal. 'That would be about the height of a trailer, wouldn't it?'

Brad nodded. 'Looks like Walter Kohler drove himself and his passengers clean off the track,' he agreed.

'Yeah, but maybe that was no bad thing!' Kirstie was quick to seize a new possibility. 'Say the trailer spun out of control and the front end smashed into the tree. Say the accident stunned the driver and the people in the cab, but left Lacey and Gunsmoke in the back unharmed.'

'That's a lot of supposin',' Brad reminded her. But he went along with the theory, listening hard and still scouting around for more clues.

Kirstie rushed ahead, hardly able to get her words out. 'So, there's the accident, then silence. Lacey knows what's happened because the whole trailer is keeled over at an angle and the ramp at the back has come loose in the crash. She can scramble to the back and peer out. She can shove at the ramp until it's lowered to the ground. Still no movement from the Kohlers in the front. So what does she do?'

'She unties the blue roan and gets him out of there pretty darn quick.' Brad took up the idea. 'That's if she's strong enough to do all this after the injury she sustained back at the cabin. Let's reckon she is. So she and Gunsmoke make it on to the road. The Kohlers are getting their act together by this time, so she has to move fast. She climbs into the saddle and takes the easiest way out of here.'

Together Brad and Kirstie turned full circle, trying to spot Lacey's supposed escape route.

'Not back the way we just came.' Brad dismissed

one choice due to the high cliffs. 'And not straight ahead because that way she'd have to ride right past the Kohlers.'

'How about this culvert?' Kirstie had spotted a narrow ravine to the left of the track. Leading Johnny down it, she found there was enough space for horse and rider, then at the far end a way out on to open scrubland through spiky yukka plants and a tangle of thorn bushes. Her eyes lit on the difficult undergrowth and on a hank of long, silver-grey hair caught in the thorns.

Brad was close behind. 'Looks like a horse lost part of his tail.' He murmured the obvious with a wry smile.

There was no need to say any more. This was it – the opportunist escape route which Lacey and Gunsmoke had chosen.

Through the culvert out on to a long slope which rolled into a shallow valley then rose again towards a solitary rock on the horizon.

Kirstie imagined the flight under a dark, cloud-laden sky, the thunder of hooves, Lacey having to trust the horse to find his way across the black terrain. Perhaps the shadow of the rock in the distance, a gleam of silver moonlight, a race to get clear of the ruthless Kohlers.

'See that rock?' Brad too noted it as the only distinctive point and therefore the likely destination for the fleeing horse and rider.

Kirstie made out the outline – like a creature lying on its back with a big belly and a pointed nose, a landmark fashioned out of massive rocks and boulders, worn down by aeons of weather to its present cartoon shape.

'Yeah, I see it,' she said quietly, preparing to mount Johnny Mohawk and ride on. 'I know that place. It's called Snoopy Rock. And I'd lay down my life that's where Gunsmoke was headed last night!'

The race across the open valley took Brad and Kirstie across scrubland dotted with the dry husks of tobacco plants, spiky yukkas, wild thyme and vivid globe cacti. Flattened by the storm, the vegetation lay pressed to the sodden yellow earth, presenting few obstacles to the charging horses.

'Why Snoopy?' Brad asked, hat jammed over his forehead, Jitterbug's hooves thundering as she came up alongside. They were half a mile from the lonely hump of rock, raising rabbits from the undergrowth and making them scoot.

'Because the outline looks like the dog in the

Peanuts strip-cartoon.' Kirstie spelled it out a touch impatiently.

'Yeah, right; like *that's* plain for any fool to see! Yee-hah!' Picking up still more speed, Brad and Jitterbug showed Johnny a clean pair of heels. Brad covered the last few hundred yards of scrubland with a show of horsemanship that a jockey in the Kentucky Derby would find hard to match.

He only slowed in the shadow of the looming rock because he received a radio signal from the ranch. By the time Kirstie caught up with him, he was already deep in conversation with Sandy Scott.

'So Larry's on his way to Bonney Lake right now,' she reported. 'But I thought you should know, Tim Foster arrived there already and checked things out again. This time he took a look in the Kohlers' barn and confirmed that Gunsmoke ain't there. Over.'

Brad replied that he and Kirstie weren't surprised. He brought the ranch boss up to date with the latest events. 'Bring Luther Irving's guys out to Snoopy Rock,' he directed. 'They can get here quicker than the Forest Rangers in their Jeeps. And maybe we'll need a doctor when we finally track Lacey down. Over.'

'There's a qualified First Aider on board Luther's chopper, and a full medical kit – so no problem.' As usual, Sandy sounded fully in control. 'But listen, Brad, there's more to come on Tim's visit to Bonney Lake. Over.'

Easing out of the saddle and leading Jitterbug towards the nearest tree, he told her to go ahead.

'So Gunsmoke never made it to Bonney Lake, but the horse-trailer did. Tim noticed it had a lot of damage to the front fender, and one corner of the roof was caved in. Over.'

'That figures! Over.' Brad gave Kirstie an excited nod, then pulled her in close to listen to the crackling radio message.

'Plus one more thing!' Even Sandy's calm voice rose as she conveyed the next piece of information. 'Tim told Larry that he took the chance to look inside the empty trailer. Walter Kohler was all for preventing him, but Tim threatened to drive right back to the sheriff's office for a search warrant, so Kohler saw sense and backed down. Over.'

'What did Tim find?' Kirstie leaned towards the radio and cut in with her question.

'A strip of cotton fabric hidden under a heap

of straw. It looked like someone had ripped off the bottom of a shirt to use the stuff as a bandage. It was stained with blood. Over.'

Kirstie gasped then bit her lip. 'Mom, this looks real bad! Over.'

'I know, honey. Tim let Walter Kohler know that he would be taking away the fabric for forensic tests. He warned him to stay put at Bonney Lake pending further developments . . .'

'Gee, that's one good thing . . .'

'No, hold it. No sooner does Tim leave Bonney Lake and report back to Larry, who as you know is already on his way, when Larry gets a second call; this time it's from Ed Jessop. Ed's the Kohlers' other hired help. He's picked up the latest and knows his boss shouldn't be leaving the house. So when he sees Walter get into his Ford Mustang five minutes after Tim has left, he knows it's time to contact the sheriff. Over.'

'Walter Kohler disobeyed the deputy's order!' Kirstie felt herself stiffen and a shiver of anxiety ripple down her spine.

'Yeah, and not only that. There's worse. According to Ed, it's what Kohler carried into the car with him that I need to tell you about.'

'What, Mom? Spit it out!'

Sandy struggled to control her voice. She delivered the bad news almost in a whisper, as if saying it out loud only confirmed the danger they suddenly found themselves in. 'Larry reckons the guy's gone crazy. He's heading this way armed with a gun!'

9

'Did you ever meet this guy, Kohler?' Brad asked Kirstie as they hitched their horses to a branch.

The race to find Lacey and Gunsmoke grew more urgent by the minute. Kirstie reckoned on maybe fifteen minutes before Meredith's father got here, presuming he could avoid Larry Francini and his deputy.

'No, never,' she acknowledged. 'Did you?'

'Sure, when Ben bought the blue roan. He took me along to look at the condition of the horse and check out whether we could pull him back into shape. Walter Kohler was the one who

131

shook hands on the deal.'

'What's he like?' Gazing up at the landmark rock, Kirstie decided that the first thing to do was to climb it and gain the best vantage point for miles around. So she began to work out hand and footholds as she listened to Brad's description of Public Enemy Number One.

'Fair haired like his daughter. He's a short guy; no more than five-four. Big problem for a man like Kohler. He wears boots with Cuban heels to add a couple of inches.'

'I don't mean what's he look like. I mean, what kind of guy is he?'

'That's what I'm trying to tell you. If you're five-four wishing you were six-two all your life, you're gonna want to prove yourself any which way you can. Kohler's into hunting elk up near Estes Park. His study is lined with trophies for fly fishing. There are college photos of him coaching the senior baseball team.'

'I get the picture.' Kirstie had worked out a route to the summit of Snoopy Rock. She set foot on a low ledge and began to heave herself up. 'So you didn't like the guy?'

Brad shrugged non-committally and went his own way around the base of the rock. 'I don't like the way he treated his horse.'

'Or the fact that the whole family lied about it.' When it came to it, Kirstie couldn't find a single good word to say about the Kohlers. Reaching for the next handhold, she continued her climb.

'Here come the rescue 'copters.' Pausing to look back down the valley, Brad made out Luther Irving's teams sweeping slowly out of the shallow dip. Their engines chugged and churned; the whir of their blades grew more distinct as they approached.

And, by the time Kirstie made it to the top of the fifty foot rock, the helicopters were landing on a narrow plateau two hundred yards away from where she and Brad stood. They settled heavily, rocking as they descended, their blades whipping up a dirt-storm which rose and drifted off towards the four-lane San Luis freeway to the south side of the landmark.

When the dust settled, Brad strode out along the plateau to greet Irving's men.

Kirstie quickly spotted that the nearest chopper contained two unexpected passengers. The first person out was the rescue team leader, but close behind were Carol and Steve Darwin.

Last seen bitching and bickering in the new

barn at Half-Moon Ranch, the real surprise for Kirstie was the look of undisguised agony on Lacey's mom's face. Gone was the cool pretence that her daughter wasn't in much danger, that Lacey was a melodramatic kid who every now and then took it into her head to give them a good scare.

Instead, Kirstie read a deep fear in the red slash of the woman's downward-turned mouth as she ran ahead of her husband to speak with Brad.

'Did you find her?' Carol gasped, clutching the sleeve of Brad's jacket. 'Say she's OK! Please!'

'We're still on the trail. We're gonna get to her real soon,' he promised, looking to the husband to calm his wife.

Steve Darwin tried to detach Carol's hands from Brad's jacket, but he failed to prise her fingers free. 'Honey,' he pleaded. 'Let the guy carry on looking. Crying and going crazy ain't gonna help none.'

'But it's all my fault!' Carol's tears spilled down her pale, strained face as Luther Irving and a woman paramedic carrying a first-aid kit quickly approached from behind. 'If I hadn't been so hard on her lately, she never would've tried this. But no; I said she had to go with the flow, accept the new situation. I didn't give her enough of my time!'

Too late now! Kirstie thought, getting a bird's eye view of the tears and regrets. But then maybe not. All it would take to make things right would be for Carol to tell Lacey this when they finally caught up with her. And for Steve Darwin to agree.

'We just want Lacey back!' Carol turned from Brad to Luther, pleading with everyone in sight. 'I want her home. I want my daughter. Please find her for me!'

Only when the paramedic stepped in to put a comforting arm around her shoulder did the distraught mother bury her face against the woman's shoulder and fall silent. This left the others free to confer with Brad, who suggested getting the choppers airborne once more so that they could scan the half-mile slope between Snoopy Rock and Route 5.

'If Kohler plans to drive his car back to the place where he had the accident with the trailer, this is the way he has to come,' he told them.

'But why would he come back?' Luther questioned the wisdom of the act.

'Man, I can't read his mind. But where else

would the guy be going with a shotgun resting across his passenger seat straight after a visit from the sheriff's deputy?'

'You got a point,' the rescue leader admitted, then quickly gave the order for his teams to return to their helicopters. Kirstie saw Steve Darwin and the paramedic help Carol back into the nearest one, heard the blades begin to churn, then turned her back away from the rising cloud of dust.

'What can you see from up there?' Brad yelled as soon as the helicopters veered away down the valley and his voice could be heard above the roar of their engines.

'Twenty miles of yukkas and cactus plants!' she cried back, her hopes dipping as she scanned the vast area beyond the freeway. 'One gas station a mile down the road. Two articulated trucks loaded with pine logs, heading for San Luis.'

'Yeah, well, c'mon down!' Brad made it clear that they were wasting time. What they needed to do was to get back on horseback and systematically carry on the ground search.

'Hey no, hold on!' A glint of sunlight reflecting in a car windshield made Kirstie hesitate. The car was stationary, parked in the turn-off to a ranch which stood close to the highway. But most of it was hidden behind a small stand of trees, the golden canopy of leaves shielding it from sight. 'Parked car!' she reported.

'Worth takin' a closer look?'

'Yep.' In her eagerness, Kirstie missed her footing and found herself sliding and scrambling down the rock almost out of control. She jumped on to the ground out of breath, legs bruised, her hands scratched to blazes.

'Do we make radio contact with the choppers?' Brad wondered, glancing skywards to see that Luther's teams were in fact making their way in the opposite direction to where the car was parked.

'Not yet. First let's see what there is to see.'

They scrambled for their horses and headed them past Snoopy, over the plateau and steadily downhill. Another truck appeared round a bend and trundled along the road, soon passed by a much faster pick-up loaded with rattling oil drums.

'We take it easy, OK?' Brad reminded Kirstie as they approached the stand of aspens. He could see from here that the ranch was called The Silver Dollar and that trees lined both sides of the wide entrance. The drive was neatly fenced, the ranch house standing half a mile down a white track. Close to the gate was an old, cylindrical water tower built on tall wooden stilts. 'We don't go galloping in like the Lone Ranger. If it looks like we're on to something, we call for back-up.'

Kirstie nodded. They were almost down to road level and still the trees hid the identity of the parked car. But another glimpse told her it was a bright colour; maybe orange, maybe red. She felt her skin prickle at the possibility that they were indeed riding towards Walter Kohler's flashy sports car.

'Red convertible!' Brad confirmed. 'That's the baby we want!'

As he spoke, Jitterbug lost her footing and stumbled down the slope. Her surprised whinny broke the silence and made Kirstie hold her breath. They could do without the horses giving notice of their approach.

But it was too late. Jitterbug was blundering on through the narrow belt of trees, whinnying again as yet another massive truck approached at speed. The silver monster roared by, sending the sorrel mare dancing across the ranch gateway until she almost collided with the parked car.

'Empty!' Brad hissed at Kirstie, leaning

sideways to take a look inside. It was a Mustang all right; the same model as Estelle Kohler had driven into the yard at Half-Moon Ranch. And, joining Brad to inspect it more closely, Kirstie could see empty gun cartridges scattered across the front seat. Her shocked face turned to Brad, inviting him to suggest the next move.

He frowned then dipped one hand into his pocket to pull out the radio. Jitterbug's hooves struck the surface of the hard shoulder as Brad walked his horse around the parked car. *Clip-clip-clip*. Her metal shoes rang out on the tarmac.

'Hold it right there!' A man with a gun stepped out from between the trees and the water tower.

In an instant Kirstie reined Johnny out of sight between some trees.

The man hadn't seen her. He turned his back and pointed the shotgun straight at Brad. 'You lookin' for me?'

'Kohler!' Shock made Brad spit out the name. But, hand still in his pocket, his gaze rested steadily on the barrel of the gun. He raised one eyebrow in scorn. 'Now you don't wanna do nothing you'd regret!'

His tone seemed to enrage the man. 'Get down!' he ordered with a jerk of the gun. 'Take

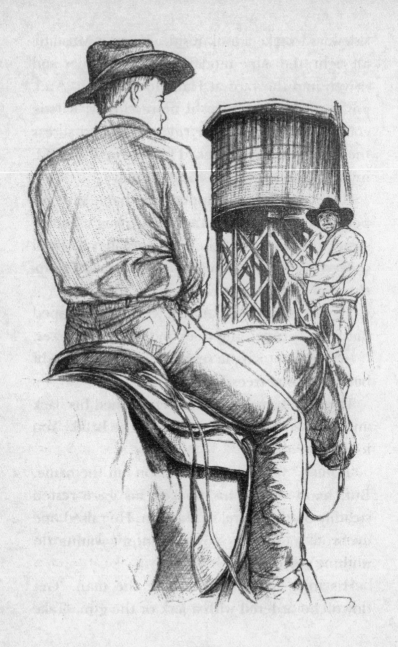

your hand out of your pocket and move nice and easy through those trees towards that water tower!'

Kirstie watched as Brad decided not to cross his opponent. *Keep quiet, Johnny. Don't make a sound!* she prayed.

'Now move it!' Kohler told Brad, who deliberately kept his eyes fixed on the gun as he dropped Jitterbug's reins and let the horse wander towards Kirstie. Kohler made sure that the long barrel kept him square in its sights every step of the way.

'You wanna play heroes?' Walter Kohler sneered, his back still to Kirstie. ' "Reining champion rescues injured girl!" A nice little story for the *San Luis Times!*'

Kirstie grabbed hold of Jitterbug as the two men stepped beween the wooden legs of the water tower. She slid from the saddle and tied both horses to the nearby fence.

'So go ahead, rescue the girl!' Kohler laughed right in Brad's face as Kirstie crept silently after them. 'She lost a little blood and blacked out a while since, but she'll probably make it after a little medical attention.'

Brad backed out of the far side of the tower,

from shadow into bright sunlight. Then he jerked sideways towards a still, slight figure propped against one of the strong stilts, head hanging, eyes closed.

Lacey! Kirstie drew breath and felt her heart thump against her ribs.

'Pity about Gunsmoke, though!' Kohler jeered, stepping between Brad and the unconscious girl. He prodded him away with the tip of the barrel, before rubbing in what to Kirstie seemed like a terrible truth.

Too late! she groaned to herself, hardly able to bear the man's sneering tone as he went on pressing Brad back with the barrel of his gun.

'That would've made a real nice headline: "Reining expert rescues injured girl *and* recaptures runaway horse!" But this ain't no fairy story, Mr Martin . . . And happy endings come more expensive in real life than the lousy couple of hundred dollars you and Ben Marsh paid me for my pretty little blue roan gelding!'

10

Say something, Brad! Kirstie needed him to distract
Kohler's attention. She knew that the guy with
the gun wasn't open to reason, but anything Brad
could do or say might give her precious seconds
to work out what action to take.

'It seemed to me you were more'n happy to
grab whatever you could for Gunsmoke,' Brad
reminded Kohler warily, his hands raised to chest
height, his eye never straying from the barrel of
the gun. 'And it didn't surprise me none. I never
saw a horse in such poor condition in my entire
life.'

Good, Brad; good! Kirstie took a deep breath and crept out from her hiding place amongst the trees. Softly she moved forward, knowing that every footfall on the stony surface at the entrance to The Silver Dollar could spell disaster.

Kohler twitched the gun in irritation, grinning nastily as the sudden action made Brad jerk backwards. 'Yeah, but you and that wrangler made a fool out of me by getting the stupid horse back into shape. To me Gunsmoke looked like he was dog food. He was sure as heck a waste of veterinary charges when we had him.'

Danger seemed to sharpen Kirstie's senses. She felt the heat of the sun burn her neck as she crept across the open land between the trees and the water tower, saw Lacey stir slightly and try to raise her head, heard the movements and snicker of an unseen horse beyond a thicket of thorn bushes some twenty yards from where Kohler and Brad stood.

So Gunsmoke *was* still alive! Maybe it wasn't too late after all.

Slowly, slowly. Don't make a sound. She heard her heart thud in her chest, her own breathing turned up full-volume inside her head.

Kohler had stopped directly under the far side

144

of the wooden tower, half his attention on Lacey's slow arousal from unconsciousness, but the gun still pointing directly at Brad. 'The easy thing would've been for you to hand the horse back over when my wife and kid came asking,' he told Brad. 'Then we wouldn't all be in this fix.'

In the distance Kirstie picked up the sound of the two rescue helicopters turning and heading back their way. Kohler heard them too and it visibly raised his stress level as he strode over to Lacey. He stooped and pulled roughly at her elbow. The girl groaned and resisted feebly.

Brad took a split-second chance to move in on them, but Kohler was already up and aiming the gun again.

Brad froze, then changed tack. 'So where's the horse now?'

'Tied up and grazing by that bush over there!' Kohler jeered. 'He's like a prisoner on death row, getting to eat his last bellyful before they pull the switch!'

'You're fixing to put a hole in the poor guy's head?' Brad asked deliberately, his gaze still steady.

Before Kohler could reply, Kirstie darted for a vertical ladder fixed to the side of the tower, leading to a narrow platform around the rim of the giant container. *Stay where you are!* she silently urged the gunman. *Don't move one step away from that spot!*

'. . . Sure I'm gonna shoot him. That's how come I'm standing here.'

Brad's eyes flickered up towards Kirstie on the ladder. 'But why?' he challenged Kohler, acting like he was about to step forward to try and stop him.

Kohler reacted by jabbing the long barrel in Brad's ribs. 'No one makes a fool out of me and walks away with the profits!'

Kirstie climbed quickly and quietly until she reached the platform. Crouching low, she eased her way around the tower until she was directly above Kohler.

Brad resisted the jabbing gun. 'Well, sorry pal. I just rode along and messed up your neat little plan! You can't shoot the horse in cold blood in front of a witness!'

'Wanna bet?' Kohler seemed actually to be enjoying the situation, proving to Brad that he could outsmart everyone. 'All I need to say is that it was a mercy killing – the horse threw his rider and went lame; no way could he be kept alive!'

'But it ain't true!' Brad protested.

'Prove it!' Kohler retorted over the growing *chug-chug-chug* of the chopper engines

Now! Kirstie told herself. *Now or never!*

She crouched at the edge of the platform, looking down on Kohler, who got ready to stride off and untie Gunsmoke, then finish off the job he'd come out here to do.

She must fall like a dead weight, land on his back, throw him off balance . . .

Ready. Lean forwards. Launch into mid-air, drop like a stone.

She free-fell on to Kohler, sending him sprawling forwards. His finger curled around the trigger of the shotgun and squeezed. A shot rang out.

'Brad, grab the gun!' Kirstie screamed at the top of her voice.

Brad threw himself forward to wrest the weapon from Kohler then flung himself full length at his legs. With Kirstie still clinging to Kohler's broad back and the aim of the gun flying wildly off target, the gunman tripped and crashed to the ground.

Afterwards, when the adrenalin rush was over

and there was time to think about what had taken place, Kirstie felt herself go weak. She had to sit right down on the ground beside the water tower and hunch forward until her head stopped spinning.

'Kirstie?' Brad's disembodied voice floated in on her consciousness from some unspecified place. 'You OK?'

'Yeah, cool.' She took a deep breath, tried to get up, buckled again at the knees.

This is crazy! she told herself. *What happened to my legs? How come there's this churning, whirring noise mushing my brain?*

Oh yeah, helicopters. Two of them descended from the blue sky. Men came running, hauled Brad off of Kohler, pinned the gunman's arms behind his back and quickly hustled him out of Kirstie's line of vision.

Then she saw Lacey stir and come slowly back to life, a streak of dark, dried blood down her pale face, two raw gashes on her forehead and cheek.

Kirstie blinked and sighed, opened her eyes. Carol Darwin was there, hovering over her daughter, imploring her to wake up, saying sorry a hundred times over.

'Lacey, honey, we love you! Don't ever try anything like this again!'

'Mom?' Lacey whispered. She didn't know where she was or what had happened. Only that Carol was there, putting her arms around her and not letting go until the paramedic finally moved in with stretcher and blankets.

'Kirstie?' Once Kohler had been safely bundled into the nearest chopper, Brad came to bend over her. 'How're you doin'?'

'Great!' *Stand up, act like this is all part of a normal day.* (Guys with guns, talk of shooting beautiful horses, a runaway girl found unconscious, rescue helicopter . . . sure, this was normal!)

'Here, let me help.' Brad offered her his hand.

'What's gonna happen to Kohler?' she gasped, swaying unsteadily as Brad raised her to her feet.

'Luther will fly him over to Larry Francini's office. They'll lay some pretty serious charges, I guess.'

Kirstie's gaze focussed on Lacey's stretcher being lifted on to the helicopter. She could see the girl struggling to sit up and call out something to her. But the chopper blades completely drowned out her words.

What a day! Her legs wobbled as she staggered towards Lacey, her mind sending flashbacks of the moment when she sprang the piggy-back trick on Kohler, the squeeze of the trigger, the crack of the gun ... 'I didn't catch what you said!' Kirstie yelled at Lacey, hair whipped back by the force of the whirling chopper blades, hands clinging to the helicopter's sliding door to keep herself upright.

Tears streamed down the injured girl's face, smearing and smudging the dried bloodstain as she gripped her mother's hand. 'I said, take care of Gunsmoke for me! Promise you won't send him back to Bonney Lake!'

Kirstie's head came clear. The world stopped spinning and a huge smile appeared on her face. 'No way!' she insisted. 'After what we all just went through, anybody who figures on taking that blue roan away from Half-Moon Ranch does it over my dead body!'

'Lacey has something she'd like to tell you,' Carol Darwin said to Sandy Scott with an embarrassed smile.

It was Sunday; three days after the injured girl had been air-lifted to hospital. The patient had been X-rayed, tested, rested and pronounced ready to go home. She and her parents had called in at Half-Moon Ranch for a final farewell.

'Go ahead, shoot.' A relaxed Sandy leaned beside Matt on the arena fence, watching Brad work with Little Vixen on a special reining move called a roll-back. The fall weather had turned kind after the mid-week thunderstorm and there was a dusky pink glow on the quiet horizon.

Leading Gunsmoke into the arena past the small group gathered by the fence, Kirstie noticed Lacey slide her hand through the crook of her mom's arm as if for moral support. Then she cleared her throat to say what was on her mind.

'Mrs Scott, I'm real sorry for the problems I caused.' She whispered with downcast eyes. 'I never meant for any of it to happen.'

'That's cool,' Sandy murmured in a warm tone. 'Really; forget it, Lacey. We got a result, didn't we?'

Kirstie paused and grinned right at Lacey before she led Gunsmoke into the arena. 'We sure did! C'mon, little guy, time to show Brad and Vixen a thing or two.'

'No, you don't understand.' Carol wasn't happy

to leave it at that. She nudged Steve in the side for him to add his explanation.

'What Carol and Lacey mean is, we don't want for you to carry on thinkin' that Lacey was runnin' away for good on Wednesday night,' he began.

Then his wife quickly stepped in again. 'Lacey knows it looks bad, and she should never have ridden out alone, but the truth is she only planned one last trip out to Hummingbird Rock on Gunsmoke as a way of saying goodbye.'

'Hey, slow down!' Kirstie led Gunsmoke back to the fence. She let the blue roan stick his head over it and nuzzle around Lacey's jacket pocket looking for treats. 'You mean you never meant to run away with him for good? You planned to ride him out and back here again all in the same evening?'

Her eyes troubled, Lacey nodded. 'Stupid idea, huh? Only, the Kohlers had to show up, didn't they? Have you ever been chased along a Jeep road at dusk by a maniac in a giant horse-trailer?'

Kirstie shook her head. 'Not lately.'

'Those headlights really spooked Gunsmoke. He saw Mr Kohler jump out of the truck and he set off like crazy for the loggers' cabin at the end of the track. The trailer soon caught up with us. Honest to God, we thought they were gonna run us down!'

'It's OK!' Kirstie interrupted. She and Brad had more or less figured the rest. Going through the actual details would only upset Lacey all over again. 'Listen, Lace. Mom, Matt and me; we think you did a real good job escaping from the Kohlers and keeping the horse out of their hands.' Especially since it turned out the poor kid had only been half conscious for most of Wednesday night, finally wandering with Gunsmoke into the shelter of Snoopy Rock.

'You do?' Lacey smiled and took a piece of candy from her pocket. 'Can I give it to him?' she asked Sandy.

But Gunsmoke didn't stand on ceremony. He darted his head forward and nipped the candy between his rubbery lips. One quick toss of the head, a gulp and it was gone.

'So you'll allow Lacey to come back to the ranch and visit us all?' Sandy was asking Mr and Mrs Darwin.

The eager horse poked his head back over the fence and nudged the empty palm of Lacey's hand.

'Just you try and stop her!' Steve Darwin joked. The week's events seemed to have jolted him out of permanent overdrive. 'Carol here plans to take next weekend off work to drive Lacey down.'

'Excellent.' Matt added his own quiet seal of approval, one eye on the dramatic sliding stop and ninety degree change of direction which Brad had just executed on Little Vixen. 'Your turn, Kirstie!' he challenged with a wry grin. 'Beat that if you can.'

'No thanks!' Kirstie had just had a better idea. She gave her own mom and Carol Darwin a quick look. Both women understood and nodded back. So Kirstie offered her new friend Gunsmoke's reins. 'Hey, Lace . . .'

Lacey creased her forehead doubtfully, then a gleam came into her brown eyes. 'Who, me?'

'Yeah, you!' Kirstie made it plain she wouldn't offer twice. She turned to Brad who was loping Vixen around the arena. 'Hey, Brad, Lacey wants to learn the roll-back!'

'I do?' She was laughing now, climbing the fence and jumping into the blue roan's saddle.

'You do!' Kirstie assured her, clipping Gunsmoke's marbled rump with the palm of her hand.

The gelding set off at a trot, head high, ears forward. His peculiar smooth gait seemed to make him float through the raised dust like a mirage in the evening light.

'Yee-hah!' Brad greeted horse and rider.

'Yee-hah!' Lacey giggled. She watched closely as Brad manoeuvred Vixen into position for another roll-back.

'Sliding stop, rein to the right, shift your weight to the same side all at the same time, OK?'

'OK!'

'Ready?'

'Ready!'

'Let's go!' Brad came first at a fast lope, straight at Kirstie and the rest. He slid Vixen's back feet under her, rolled her away and galloped her on.

Lacey tried it on Gunsmoke. Slide – skid – roll away to the right and gallop off. The gelding's action was precise and elegant, the whole routine perfect.

'Yee-hah!' Brad cried.

'Yee-hah!' she yelled back.

'Your girl sure can ride,' Sandy told a proud Carol and Steve Darwin.

Watching Lacey's radiant face, Kirstie felt pretty good too.

'That Brad ain't exactly a clunk in the saddle neither,' Matt commented quietly, winking at his mom and Kirstie as he sauntered away towards the corral.

'Did you hear . . . ? Am I imagining . . . ?' Sandy's mouth dropped open. The two riders in the arena talked through their next routine.

'I did hear. And no you're not imagining things!' Kirstie laughed out loud. 'Believe me; your son just said something nice about your boyfriend!'

Sandy flustered and coloured up as Brad and

Lacey rode by. 'He's not my boyfriend!' she hissed.

Kirstie eyeballed her.

'OK, then. He is. Oh my!'

As her mom retired with the Darwins in a heap of girlish blushes, Kirstie's grin nearly split her face in two. Then she settled in to watch Brad jump on to Gunsmoke and demonstrate a sliding stop, followed by a roll-back, followed by a perfect three hundred and sixty degree spin.

. . . *No fooling around. Right on.*

Another Hodder Children's book

HORSES OF HALF-MOON RANCH
Golden Dawn

Jenny Oldfield

Golden Dawn, a sorrel mare, gives birth to
a foal, Tatum. But when flash floods pour
down from the mountains, they wreak
havoc in the meadow and little Tatum goes
missing. Could the foal have survived the
flood? Kirstie and Golden Dawn set off
downriver to find out. Ahead lies danger –
sub-zero night temperatures, coyotes and
mountain lions, and of course the ever
present threat of another disastrous
flood . . .